I0629414

Brittney Stewart

THE LAST OF THE

DYING

Brittney Stewart

THE LAST OF THE
DYING

Unusual Publishing

The Last of the Dying

First Edition Copyright © 2010 Brittney Stewart

Third Edition Copyright © 2016 Brittney Stewart

Cover Design © 2016 Brittney Stewart

This is a work of fiction. All names, places, and scenarios are used fictitiously, or as the product of the author's imagination.

This book or any portion thereof
may not be reproduced or used in any manner whatsoever without the express written permission of the author, except for the use of brief quotations in a book review.

All rights reserved. Published in the United States of America by Unusual Publishing.

ISBN-13: 978-0692644355

ISBN-10: 0692644350

ONE

It was the earliest part of the morning and the blazing sun was just beginning to rise over the flat, dead line of the horizon. The unmistakable feeling of a dying world crept through the lonely streets – streaking across every black window, and over every dying over-grown lawn.

Most of the houses on this quiet street were empty, their owners having left weeks, even months ago, when the fate of the world was definite. Even though hundreds of thousands were already gone, more still remained, saving all the money they could and holding onto any hope of leaving.

In a grimy-looking house sitting on the very edge of the street, there was a man standing behind the blackness of a window looking out at the orange orb rising into the sky. It was the same routine every day for him and for every other stuck on earth; deserted and left to die.

Silas was one of the unfortunate lower middle-class who had no choice but to stay. Leaving would cost, and it would cost more than he had ever dreamed of having. As he stared across the mostly deserted street he noticed a flicker from a nearby window. He blinked, peering through the cracks and streaking fog he saw shadows moving quickly in its depths.

Suddenly he felt the ground shaking as the silence was broken by a blast of engines roaring. Silas knew what it was before he saw it. The grass on both sides of the street waved violently as bits of dead foliage flew across his yard, tangling up in the fence.

Many of the remaining neighbors stepped out to watch as a massive flying beast landed in the center of the street. It resembled a helicopter with two giant blades on top allowing the machine to land virtually anywhere. It also had four wings, each with its own powerful jet.

When the roaring finally died down, a family stepped out of the very house Silas had been watching only seconds before the aircraft had landed.

A couple and one small child clutching a stuffed owl walked to the Hilo lift, wind whipping their hair. Each of the little girl's parents carried their own heavy bag as they climbed aboard the enormous craft. Suddenly the engines started up again sending debris flying everywhere. Just as it began to lift off the ground, Silas noticed a woman running down the street toward the Hilo lift as fast as she could manage.

He wanted to look away but it was too late, one of the Rescuers had already pulled out one of their special weapons of submission.

In a matter of seconds the woman was lying flat on the ground, completely still. Silas froze, wondering if acting out would be a mistake. It seemed as though in that moment Silas's brain was having a war – both left and right sides of the battle pulling him toward a separate fate.

Milliseconds later the screams erupted. Cries of pain and fury blended together sending a shock wave through the street. Silas ran for the door where he froze at the sight before him. The street had turned into a battle scene.

A few figures that Silas recognized were charging down the street toward the ship, their faces blurry behind the shield bubble that protected them from attack. Silas dove from the doorway, taking no time to think he rushed toward his friends. The Hilo lift rose further into the air and so did the weapons held tightly in the fists of ten guards ready to stun. In an instant several more bodies fell to the ground near the unconscious women. Silas pushed through the crowd searching for her; he saw nothing but a blur of panic and the screaming of a hundred desperate souls.

In the seconds that had passed since Silas entered the battle only a few remained standing in the street. Silas recognized a flash of extremely large black hair and darted forward, throwing himself inside of the shield bubble. The pain that shot across the left side of his face was excruciating. He looked around dizzily for the cause, but he seemed to be having trouble keeping his eyes in the right spot.

"Silas!" The high voice pierced his throbbing brain, bringing him back from the daze. "What are you doing in here?"

Terra was standing only a few inches from him holding a shock stick in her hands. Silas would have laughed if his head had not been hurting so badly.

"Are you trying to kill me or something?" He grunted rubbing his sore head.

"I don't have time for this!" Terra said impatiently, pushing him behind her and moving forward to join the remaining bubbles.

Silas walked closely behind her in the cramped space looking through the shield at the dark shadow rising higher into the air; it turned slowly facing the sky as it prepared for flight.

"Take this and don't move, I'm going to pop over and visit Finx." Terra was already half-way out of the shield before Silas could protest.

He looked down at his scarred hands wound tightly around the base of the very weapon that had given him such a headache, and sighed. Whatever Terra was up to, he was sure it meant trouble.

TWO

The parade had been going for days. People standing in the streets waved their hands through the crystal clear air of NB1. NB1, or New Blue one, was called home by nearly one million people. It had been such a success that a second was already in the making. Vadell Monroe was hurrying through the crowd, pushing her way to the front row. The ground was already shaking when she spotted the tiny dot in the sky.

"It's coming! I can see it!" Someone yelled as the crowd erupted into applause and whistles. Another family had been saved from certain death by the Rescue Team. The Hilo lift landed gracefully onto the landing pad, which caused another outburst of squeals from the audience. Vadell watched as streamers and balloons dashed through the air from the force of the Hilo's blades. The roar of the engines could barely be heard over the crowd as they welcomed the new family.

It was not until the ground stopped trembling that Vadell noticed the family was already getting out of the Hilo lift, their faces smiling brightly at the warm welcome. The new settlers had been moving in for almost eight months, but the parade would continue for anyone new.

The new arrivals were becoming fewer, and the time between those arrivals would be days sometimes weeks. When NB1 was first completed, hundreds of people would be moved in a day. But now the numbers were thinning and Vadell was beginning to worry about the rest of them – the people left behind.

The Rescue Team had promised to save as many as they could from what was left of planet earth, but reports had claimed that it was too dangerous for the RT to land in most areas, leaving people stranded indefinitely. A tap on the shoulder brought Vadell back. She spun around quickly, trying to hide her suspicious thoughts from her mother, whom she was quite sure could read minds.

"Gah! You scared me!" Vadell gave her mother a half-smile attempting to look at least a little happy about the new arrivals.

"I'm sorry honey, but we have to go. George and I have a meeting, and the new family is going to need someone to show them around."

She was talking very fast and Vadell was only half-listening. For the first time she was starting to notice that something was wrong. All of the excitement from the move, watching some of the greatest scientists in the world change the future, it had all been a distraction from something far more dangerous. It was hanging over their heads and nobody had seen it coming.

***

The rest of the day Vadell tried unsuccessfully to avoid the thoughts that had plagued her constantly since the first sign of trouble.

The next morning she woke to the sound of the television in the next room going on about the new family, and the RT that were supposedly searching for refugees but having no luck.

"Sweetie, I'm going to the office, but I will be back for dinner. Would you pick something up?" Vadell's mother chirped as she sailed through the room to open the curtains.

"Uh, yeah no prob..." Vadell mumbled rolling over.

"OK then, see you later dear." Her mother

leaned down and kissed her on the forehead before rushing out again, leaving the light aroma of perfume and coffee behind her. Finally, when Vadell stumbled into the kitchen in search of breakfast, she noticed the TV was still on and blaring something about the rescue efforts.

The holographic screen was flashing images of buildings and trees on fire, along with giant cracks where the earth had caved in. Next it showed a member of the RT running through the rubble in a flame suit and mask carrying a limp body in his arms.

"Another life saved today by the dedicated men and women of the Rescue Team. 11 year-old Timothy Bradwell was pulled from the fiery wreckage of his home today. He was the last sole survivor of a city plagued by wildfires."

Vadell sighed and pressed the *TV Off* button on the kitchen counter. The newscast disappeared immediately leaving nothing but a blank wall and a quiet kitchen.

After breakfast, Vadell locked the house, which was a bit of a struggle with the new security system, and then headed out.

Her car set in the driveway, tiny and electric it seated only two people. She unplugged the car from its charging spot in the light post before driving out onto the quiet streets.

Vadell's parents owned a car manufacturing company that was trying to build safe and efficient cars for the new planet. Because mankind had played such a large role in the destruction of the earth, ensuring the safety of the new planet was vital; and the first step was creating low, or no emission cars.

Vadell was given her own demo car to drive. Of course not everyone was happy about this; in fact, most people thought it was unfair for Vadell to be one of the only individuals on the planet to have a car. But Vadell's parents had insisted, and after all she did *like* the car.

She drove down the clean plastic streets wondering if it would stay that way. Trillions of dollars went into making a copy of the original that was destroyed, *but this time it would be better right? We would not make the same mistakes over again.*

When she pulled into the supermarket there was a group of men wearing gray uniforms installing electric car charging docks into the side of light posts. One of the men waved as she passed.

Vadell was still having a hard time adjusting to the new supermarkets, everything was digital and it was impossible to shoplift – not that she had ever tried to test it out. Shopping was different, you still had to walk through the aisles, but it was nothing like the way people shopped in the old days. Vadell browsed the produce aisle looking over holograms of various fruits and vegetables.

She stretched out her fingers and touched the hologram of a bright red apple. A price flashed and then she pressed buy, it beeped once before going back to the hologram of the apple.

When she was done, Vadell approached the check-out and waited until her name appeared above one of the red and blue counters. She walked up and waved her hand across the sensor, it beeped and then a compartment opened and out slid a small hover board that was stacked with her groceries.

Vadell walked back to her car, the little hover board wheezing along behind her. When she had relieved the board of its burden she turned to slide the door shut, but stopped suddenly when she felt something bump her leg.

She looked down to see the tiny hover board rearing back for another blow when she realized that she had forgotten the tip.

"Okay, okay!" She yelled at the hover board, it wiggled a little before settling. She eyed it suspiciously, then held her hand out in front of her as the hover board moved forward.

A blast of light shot up from the board and engulfed her hand in sparkling yellow rays. The board beeped and then turned, zooming back to the market doors that slid open as it approached.

When she finally settled into her car it was still early – nearly 11:00am, so she decided to take lunch to her mother at the office. Vadell turned onto the big highway, the one that was still under construction. Yellow and orange lights marked roads that were blocked or not accessible to the public.

Vadell slowed her car and pulled into the vast parking lot outside the car factory. One side of the building was made entirely of glass, which stretched all the way to the top. Little blasts of steam shot up from pipes connected to the highest part of the roof.

Vadell watched as the steam twisted around in the air forming odd shapes. She thought it was beautiful how the sun bounced off the black glass, sending little rays through the air. Vadell got out of her car; walking across the parking lot she spotted the lifts.

There were three of them setting side-by-side, each glowed with the same metallic silver. She approached the closest one and the door slid open for her.

Once she was inside and the door was firmly closed she took a deep breath and said, "Third floor."

The lift shot up instantly – causing her to stumble back against the wall. Vadell was gripping the handrails so tightly that her fingers turned white, then the lift stopped.

When the doors opened she bolted out as quickly as she could, landing in a quiet hallway with red carpet. The smell of copy ink and artificial cherry floated around her head. Above each door was a holographic sign that depicted a picture of the office's owner and the slogan of the day.

Vadell walked down the hall until she came to a glossy wooden door with a picture of her mother floating above it, smiling and waving her well-manicured hand. As she approached the door a group of words appeared underneath her mother – printed in bright yellow, it read:

The human mind is like a parachute; it only functions when it is open.

Vadell waved her hand in front of the sensor smiling to herself as the door slid open. She stepped in and the door closed behind her with a soft snapping noise.

As soon as she walked in she could hear her mother's voice speaking with someone. Since there was no reply, Vadell assumed it was a digital caller. She stopped before turning the corner, the sound of her mother's voice clearer than before.

"But it isn't right for them to take that choice away. It may as well be murder!"

She sounded breathless and her voice cracked a little. There was silence for a moment and then she continued.

"I understand what is happening perfectly, but you do not. Sooner or later they are going to find out, and when they do, you will be the one to suffer." The silence swelled for a while before Vadell heard a beep – the call had ended.

Vadell grabbed her bag and turned, forgetting lunch, forgetting everything. *What was happening, and who exactly were "they"? What were "they" going to find out?* Her mind was racing when she finally made it to her car. Vadell was certain now that something was happening behind the scenes, and that her mother was involved. It all seemed too real, it was cruel validation of the suspicions she already had.

THREE

It was difficult to say for certain – impossible to pick exactly what it was that made him completely in love with her. Something about her hair that was always in tangles, and her constant planning for the future that they *might* have made him crazy. She insisted that he stay, and he wanted to, but it was pointless. She said nothing as he packed his bag, but he could feel her disapproval radiating through the back of his skull.

"If you leave, you leave alone." Her voice was weak as she spoke – a finality that he had never heard from her.

"I know what I'm doing Terra." Silas kept his back to her, avoiding her eyes – he refused to face them. "And you know as well as I do that we won't make it unless I go."

It was silent for a moment before a small hand wound around his, turning him to face her. He looked down at their feet. One glance would end everything he had been working for, all of the courage he had built up in himself – gone. Silas felt a cold chill slide into his stomach as she raised their joined hands to kiss his gently. He kept his eyes on the ground knowing that she understood. She would not put him through that pain today.

He listened to the door close quietly back in its frame. It was a miserable sound; the sound of the empty loneliness that she left behind. He swore he would never hear that sound again – He would come back because he had to, because if he did not, she would be gone forever.

FOUR

Silas was kneeling behind the perimeter of the facility, his fingers laced through the cold chain link fence, his eyes scanning the grounds for the patrol car. Finally he caught sight of lights illuminating the eastern wall just seconds before they disappeared.

The night was a quiet one, as usual. Not even the slightest breeze dared to blow through the dying trees. But this unnerving absence of sound was becoming typical. It had been years since the last bird flew through the sky, and people had adjusted to it. Silas never liked the eerie silence; it gave him the feeling that something bad was going to happen.

When he was sure of his solitude behind the protection of the fence, Silas pulled hard forcing himself up and over the side of the barrier. He landed on the dry dead grass with a soft crunch, and then darted behind the nearest tree.

Peering through the bare tree limbs toward the entrance, Silas spotted a guard standing in front of the doors holding a wireless device. The man did not seem to be interested in anything outside of his virtual world. Silas grinned to himself as he pulled the black hood over his head, reveling in how easy it was going to be.

The people here would not be worried about someone breaking in, they were convinced that the people left on earth were too busy trying to find a way out. Nobody would have time for breaking and entering, especially when it came to a facility that held no meaning to the public.

When the moment seemed right, Silas threw his head forward and ran through the trees to the western wall. He was running full speed toward a huge log lying across his path, and just as he jumped he saw it.

A massive black dog was lying just behind the log. Silas was already flying over the dog when they spotted each other. Silas felt the teeth on his ankle before he touched the ground.

Searing pain shot through his leg as the weight of the dog pulled him to the ground. Silas bit his lip to keep from wailing in pain, but it was too late, the guard had heard the struggle and was coming to investigate. He burst through the darkness, a rusty old flashlight in hand; he looked utterly shocked. Kicking and flailing on the ground, Silas tried hard to think of a way out. He reached for his bag, but it was too far away — its contents had spilled across the ground.

His hands spread out; searching for something, anything in the darkness that could be useful. He found nothing apart from two handfuls of dead grass. The guard moved closer, shock radiating from his sallow face.

"Don't move sir!" He yelled sheepishly, "Zoe, down girl, release!" He ordered the dog and her massive jaws finally loosened, releasing his mangled leg.

Silas froze, his heart beating, sweat dripping down his face. The guard walked slowly toward him as the black dog growled softly from the darkness. Silas could see only the shine that her yellow, unblinking eyes cast from the dim glow of the guards prehistoric flashlight. Suddenly Silas knew exactly what to do.

These guards were not trained for physical violence, only the Rescue Team used force. They were here for intimidation, the only weapon they had was a single electric silencer and a flashlight. The guard removed the silencer shakily from its holster along with a very old fashioned pair of hand cuffs. Silas kept his breathing steady as the guard approached – not breaking eye contact.

"Don't you move sir, I'm armed!" Silas looked at him innocently, standing completely still.

When the guard finally reached him, Silas noticed the flashlight dangling from a holster. In one movement he grabbed the flashlight and the guards arm, pulling him down to the ground Silas hit him once with the flashlight. The hard plastic bounced off of the man's skull with a sickening crack. He dropped the silencer and rolled over clutching his head. As soon as the guard went down the black dog charged at Silas, her teeth glowing white in the dark.

Silas grabbed the silencer and turned for her, but she was already on him, her teeth snapping inches from his face, her hot breath burning his eyes. IIis arm was the only thing stopping her from devouring his face. Silas knew he couldn't hold her off for long; the dog was heavy and strong.

He gathered his strength and shoved hard, pushing her back several feet. He aimed and shot twice at the dog, she collapsed instantly, the silencer had done its job.

Two small needles protruded through the dog's shiny black coat – this would keep her in an unconscious state until the needles were removed. The guard had already crawled halfway toward the entrance when Silas noticed him. He started to stand when he saw Silas approaching, but stumbled and fell back to the ground clutching his head.

Silas pointed the silencer and shot once. The guard fell. Silas took his badge and passkey, and then wiped the sweat away from his face. Silas stumbled toward the entrance, his destroyed leg wobbled under him dangerously.

He quickly swiped the passkey and the door slipped open to an old-looking building with gray chipped wallpaper. The dirty tiled floors made it impossible to detect the original color scheme hidden beneath the layers of grime.

It was nothing like he had expected, but it appeared empty so he walked carefully down the hall searching for the lab. He knew they would have to store *it* here, it was too dangerous to move to the new planet. They were convinced that nobody even knew of its existence, so it made sense that the security system would be less than perfect.

He was no longer worried about the guards; none of them were dangerous enough to harm him.

But the RT and their leader would visit from time to time in order to make sure everything was running smoothly. If Silas was unfortunate enough to be here when they were, it would mean the end.

The building itself was a mixture of old and new technology. The walls appeared old and shabby, but the doors were new, solid steel and locked with passkey technology. Of course this was not the most advanced technology, but it was strong enough to deter most.

And with the *guards* roaming around, nobody would dare try breaking in. Silas found the door at last, a plaque at the top read *Lab Personnel Only: Do Not Enter.* Under that, a yellow sign warned *CAUTION: Highly Toxic Material.* Silas smiled, he had found it. But the question remained; *what would he do with it once he got it out?*

FIVE

"GET UP! HURRY V!" Vadell woke to the blasting sound of the TV and one very anxious best friend. "Hurry V! They are talking about Sam's house!" Vadell shot up at the mention of Sam and stared around.

Lync was standing beside the bed arms folded, a deep crease between her eyebrows – the kind of expression she only wore for serious matters.

Vadell stood up and followed her toward the kitchen. The scene on the TV was a mess; fire flying across the screen, the sound of tortured screams blasted through the speakers. The sound vibrated down Vadell's spine, into the pit of her stomach.

"Today four more houses were lost in the fire, Rescue Team workers attempted to save the trapped and wounded, but unfortunately seven individuals were lost. According to sources, the Rescue Team was able to retrieve three people from the inferno. No word on the names of these individuals."

"And now we have new information on several new families arriving today..." Vadell and Lync looked at each other in awestruck silence. Footage from the wreckage had revealed a street all too familiar to both of them. It was the same street that her friend Sam lived on, and the same street that Vadell herself had lived on before moving to NB1.

Vadell folded her arms on the kitchen table and buried her face. Everything was going wrong. Sure they could try to keep saving people, but eventually everyone left there was going to die – *Sam could be one of those people.*

It was the same street she had grown up on, where she learned to ride a bike, and where she had jumped out of her two story window when she was fifteen. It was home, but now it was all destroyed. Vadell knew it could not be a natural disaster, not this quickly.

Everything was fine when she left but now it was all gone – burned away into ash. She felt a small warm hand on her back as she took a deep breath.

"He's okay V, I know he is." Lync said quietly.

"You can't be sure of that! He could be dead!" Vadell took another deep breath through her nose, realization flooding into her brain.

"But it's Sam! You know he's a survivor! If anyone could make it off that dead abyss it would be him." Lync sounded so certain of this that Vadell almost believed her.

But the cruelty of her world was crashing down on her. *How could people be this way?* Leaving their brothers, cousins, friends, sisters – their families behind to die, all to save their own necks.

The ground shook then and Vadell looked up from the table. Through the window she could see the landing pad, crowds of people packed together waving their arms and cheering. The Hilo lift was taking off again. The RT members on board waved at the crowd like the heroes everyone thought they were.

SIX

The door slid open making no sound at all. Everything was neat and clean; the shelves were lined with jars and tubes, each having their own holographic label floated above in the empty space. Some contained shiny silver liquid, in others, yellow and red spots floated in circles around each other like oil in water.

Animals were caged and stacked neatly one on top of the other in rows. Whatever animal or plant life left on earth came here to be used for experimentation and cloning. Some of the scientists where actually trying to save these animals, while others just saw them as a danger to the new world, one that could not be allowed to live. But they would not be wasted, these animals would be used as science projects.

Silas approached one of the cages cautiously, being careful not to touch anything. A small furry mammal was curled in the corner, breathing hard. Most of the cages were empty, apart from a few small animals curled up in beds of hay or shredded paper. Silas noticed a few of the cages were not cages at all, but plastic containers. Each surrounded by blue lights and yellow holograms that read *Hazardous Material: Highly Toxic.*

Moving closer, Silas saw a hairless rat scurrying around inside one of the plastic containers. The little rat stopped suddenly and looked up at him with a curious expression – his nose twitching.

Silas thought he noticed something different about the little rat; something gleamed there in the tiny box. And then he saw the eyes. They were definitely different; the iris was a very light, dead-looking brown. The color reminded him of dead grass.

The pupil was a swirl – not just a swirl, but a swirl of tentacles reaching out in all directions. And to his astonishment they were moving. Each little tentacle seemed to have its own life, moving around completely on its own inside the rat's eye.

The rat stood completely still, frozen, though not out of fear. They stared at each other for what seemed like hours before it turned and moved back to the shadows. Silas blinked and looked up at the changing holographs, each moving animatedly.

First a warning, then a strange image unlike anything he had seen before. It was a staff with two snakes curled tightly around it – hands spread out on either side like wings, and a face seemed to be looking back at him.

A disgusting-looking eyeball sat at the top, gazing around the room. The slide-show continued, and then Silas was reminded that he was not alone in the building.

Footsteps were coming quickly down the tiled hallway. Silas panicked, looking around for a hiding place. His heart jumped into his throat, he could not believe his luck! One of the metal cabinets was cracked; the door was open waiting for him.

He threw himself into the cabinet closing the door swiftly. The room was quiet for a few seconds, and then he heard the beeping of a door opening and closing again. It was the sound of the lab door on the other side of the room.

He could hear the sound of voices now, muffled by the thick metal of the cabinet. It sounded like two men arguing, but he could not hear them clearly enough to know what they were saying. There would be no way to open the cabinet without alerting them of his hiding spot.

After the rumble of voices had died down, Silas waited in the cabinet for a few minutes before opening the door and sneaking into the now empty lab.

He headed toward the computers, the one nearest one turned on when he approached, but the screen was a blank. The retina security dock blinked; blue lights flying in all directions. Silas slammed his hand on the wooden desk in frustration. Though getting into the lab had gone the way he planned, he had underestimated the security inside.

"Brilliant isn't it?" The voice made him jump to the side, grabbing his stolen silencer.

A man stood casually in front of him, arms crossed, gray hair thinning slightly on top. He took a deep breath and ran a hand down his speckled red and black tie.

"You know this is definitely not the best place to be caught snooping. If they find you here they will keep you here, and it most certainly will not be fun."

The man turned and pulled a white lab coat from the collection by the door. He heaved the coat on while he walked forward. Silas raised the gun and pointed it at the man's chest without hesitation.

"You won't need that here my friend." The man said looking at the gun. "If they want to take you down they can do it easy enough – with or without the gun."

Though the man was a total stranger, Silas felt as though he should trust him. For the first time in his life he wanted to trust a stranger. The feeling confused him, and he hesitated.

Slowly, he put the gun back in his pocket wondering what the next step would be. *How would he get out again?* Surly they had noticed the wounded guard by now and they would be looking for an intruder.

"Who are you? Why aren't you having me arrested?" Silas asked quickly.

"Because, I want to ask you for a favor." The man's face turned serious as they looked at each other.

"What do you mean a favor?" Silas asked. Then suddenly the man walked forward and stretched out his hand. Silas looked at it suspiciously before taking it with his own.

"My name is Franklin Hawes, and I want you to save the world."

SEVEN

The following week had been much the same as the previous on NB1, but Vadell was becoming more aware of the details. The pathetic news stories about fire and death, bombings and riots. Nothing was real anymore; it was all as fake as the new planet.

Everyone was walking around clueless, not knowing or caring what was happening on a planet that they had called their own.

Vadell came home at five o'clock just as her mother was sitting down for her dedicated news watching, and worrying time. She moved toward the kitchen trying to avoid the TV. She couldn't take anymore, not after Sam.

The thought of him made her heart sink again. They had never been together as a couple, but the thought of more was always there. It was just something that never really happened.

And now that he was almost certainly gone from her life, the mere thought of him made her feel like her heart was being ripped apart. She took a deep breath as she moved into her room. Throwing her things on the floor, she collapsed faced down on the bed burying her face in the fluffy comforter. She could not stop thinking about the house, the bed, everything that she had safe and sound while her friends were dying. The thought made her sick.

She laid her head sideways on the pillow, looking straight at the bedside table. Her alarm clock was spinning and twirling gracefully around in circles with silent flashing colors. Holograms always danced when someone walked in, they were built for entertainment.

The alarm clock swirled again, causing a piece of stray paper to fly off the table and float to the floor. Vadell leaned over the side of the bed, watching the paper drift until it landed on the floor. Her heart jumped, there was something written on it and it most definitely was not her handwriting.

She picked up the paper quickly and ran her eyes across the thick messy writing. Her heart thudded hard again, and she swore for a moment it stopped beating. She read through the letter quickly two more times before leaping up and grabbing her bag from the floor.

She flew through the kitchen gripping the letter tightly in her fist. She was already closing the door before her mother had taken a breath to ask her what was wrong.

**

Vadell was looking seriously at Lync who looked back with a curious expression. She waited patiently as Vadell pulled the crumpled letter from her pocket and unfolded it. Smoothing out the wrinkles she passed it to Lync who began to read it aloud:

"Vadell, don't believe anything they say, we are still here and we are fighting back. We won't last much longer, they are planning something big. I can't give you the details in case this is intercepted. Please help us, we need you. You are the only one in this world or another, who could help stop this thing before it gets out of control. "

Lync stopped there and looked up, her face white and her mouth hanging open. She looked exactly how Vadell felt inside. She bent her face back down to the letter.

"One more thing V, don't show this to anyone

except Lync, she needs to know we are still alive. Please be safe." Lync paused and raised her head to look at Vadell before saying the last word.

"*Sam.*"

EIGHT

Silas laughed one broken croak of a laugh before his face went serious again. The two stared at each other, Silas wondered if it had been a joke, or if Franklin was merely holding him there until the RT could come and arrest him. But then Franklin spoke.

"We are constructing an organism that will increase the mental capacity of human beings. This being said, I would like to use you as our first human test."

"You want to experiment on me, you mean." Franklin was walking toward him now, and Silas took a step back as he spoke.

"Well yes, but if the bonding is successful, we will be able to use you to take back the world that is ours. Think about it." And Silas was thinking about it, but it sounded ridiculous.

"How could one person stop all of them? The Rescue Team, the government, they are so strong."

"Not as strong as everyone believes them to

be. Not everything is as it seems you know..." His words faded as he looked at the hologram clock floating above the caged animals.

"You need to make a decision, because when the doctor comes back I will not be able to stop what he does with you."

"No, I can't. I can't take the chance that I might die. There are people counting on me to get them out of here."

"Then do the right thing, get them out of here. But you and I both know you cannot make it alone. If you just let us work on you. You could be stronger, faster. You could help them escape. You could help all of us escape."

Silas's mind was racing – *would it be worth the risk?* He thought of the families left behind, the children who had no choice but to sit by and watch their friends, parents, and grandparents leave thcm behind.

"If I do it, will you promise me that if I die, if the experiment fails, you will do everything you can to get these people off of this planet – will you try to save them?" They stared at each other; Franklin's eyebrows came together in a bunch at the center of his forehead.

"I will." He whispered, and then suddenly Silas heard the sound of footsteps in the hall.

The next thing he knew, he was lying on the ground with his face pushed against the stainless steel floor. It was cold against his cheek and he could feel someone's hands grabbing his wrists, locking them in a tight vice.

"Give him three doses for now." Said a gruff voice from someplace above.

The prick of a big needle cleared his head a little and he turned around to see what was happening. But a hand pushed his head back down with incredible force sending a wave of pain through his skull.

"Wherever did you find him Hawes?" said the low voice again.

"He broke into the lab sir." It was quiet in the room for a moment and then a shiny black shoe landed in front of his face.

"What is your name boy?" Silas felt a wave of annoyance shoot through his spine at being called a boy.

He always looked younger than he was. The man prodded him in the back once with something sharp. But Silas didn't answer the question, everything was getting fuzzy.

"What is your name?" The voice shouted so suddenly that everything else in the room seemed dead quiet. In fact, it was too quiet, and everything was getting dark – he seemed to be leaving the lab behind.

A green pasture was forming in front of him. Large figures were passing over the grass wearing long, black, hooded cloaks that billowed as they glided forward. The phantasms floated along paying no attention to him as he walked amongst them. He looked for a face under each cloak but found nothing but a vast pool of darkness.

The ground shook and he fell over onto the plush green grass. Looking up at the sky he saw it. A massive fireball was flying toward him out of the clear blue sky.

Large flickers of fiery death were shooting out and falling to the ground around him. He tried to run, but it was coming too fast. The hooded figures took no notice of the death that was approaching.

NINE

"It's a joke right?" Vadell leaned forward putting her elbows on her knees. "You don't think he is actually alive do you?" Lync looked completely insulted by this and stood up to pace around the room.

"Listen V, I know you come up with some crazy notions, but this is the dumbest thing you have ever said. OF COURSE HE IS ALIVE!" She stopped and stared at Vadell, frowning a little.

"I'm just saying how could it be real? How could he get a letter to me? If everyone is out to get him..."

"But they are not all out to get him V! There are thousands of people still left there. Any one of them could have a friend in the RT."

Lync threw her arms in the air and then let them smack back down to her sides.

"Listen, if he is really alive and he needs my help, I am going to help him. But how could I? He thinks that I am some hero and I'm not a hero. I am here on this planet with everyone else sitting around while people die!" They looked at each other and then Vadell looked away. "We need proof that he is still out there."

"Isn't this letter proof enough!?" Lync threw the letter at her. She felt anger welling up. Lync was supposed to be her friend – she was supposed to help her, not fight her.

"Okay listen, if you are one hundred percent certain that Sam is alive and that he is the one who sent me this, then let's go! We sneak on the next convoy and go find him ourselves." She was breathing hard now, and her head was starting to ache.

Lync didn't say a word. She turned and pulled out a pile of papers that were stacked behind her. She threw them on the table along with a backpack.

"If we are going to sneak on one of those convoys, we need to get supplies first. Also, I think you need to go to work with your mom tomorrow."

Lync began stacking the papers into groups.

"Why do I need to go there?"

"Don't they manufacture those Hilo crafts?"

"They manufacture everything that moves."

Vadell said. She was watching Lync go through an old atlas, her nose almost touching the pages.

"Exactly, we need to find out how these Hilo crafts work. We need to find a cargo hold or someplace where we can hide for the trip."

"OK, so I go with her. What will you be doing?"

Lync raised her head and grabbed the small black backpack. "I am going to get tools, and you know... basic necessities." Vadell raised her eyebrows.

"What kind of necessities, Lync?" Lync had just opened her mouth to speak when her mother knocked on the door.

"Lyncee Lou! I need you downstairs please!" Her mother's high pitched girly voice floated through the room. Vadell watched Lync's eyebrows come together again over her dark blue eyes.

"One minute mother!" Lync shouted back then turned to Vadell. "You will find out soon enough."

***

It took Vadell a few minutes before she managed

to get all of the stuff out of the car. Lync had given her several stacks of maps to study, along with a blank notebook. Vadell spent the whole evening pouring over the maps. Some of the places she recognized, others she had never seen. And Sam could be anywhere; the earth was big after all.

Lync had insisted that they both memorize as much as they could because they wouldn't be able to carry the maps with them. And if they were going to be looking for Sam, they needed at least a little bit of direction. It would do them no good to be wandering around on a dangerous planet for weeks with no direction at all.

She picked up one of the bigger atlases and cracked it open. The crinkled letter floated out and landed on her lap. Lync must have put it in there before she left. Vadell considered this as she ran her eyes across the chunky writing.

It seemed silly that she had doubted the authenticity of the letter. It was Sam, every word, every smudge in the ink. She could see him writing it in her head, his long black hair falling in his face as he scribbled quickly.

She missed Sam, she missed him a lot. It seemed like every time they were apart the world started to look different, and not for the better. He had made everything in her life seem clearer. He made her realize things about herself that she was too scared to notice. When she had read until her eyes burned, she closed the books and packed them neatly away.

She laid Sam's letter back on the bedside table and began to wonder how it had found its way to her room in the first place.

Obviously he had known someone who could smuggle it to NB1 – *but how did he get it to her? How would he know which house? How did he get it past security?* It was hours before she finally fell asleep, questions still rolling along inside her head.

TEN

Silas's face was burning when he woke. The bright light shining in his eyes made him think that the fire had been real after all. Voices were floating in the room, bouncing off the walls and swimming through his ears. Everything sounded fuzzy like his head was full of cotton. He flexed his muscles to move, everything hurt. He was sore and aching in every muscle and tendon.

He tried to move his arms, but they were being held down by something, he tried his legs too with no success. Silas doubted he could have moved anyway, he was extraordinarily weak.

He tried hard to think back to the last thing he remembered, but his brain blurred every time he got close to an answer. It was nice to just relax and think about nothing, it felt peaceful. But the more he lay there the feeling that he had forgotten something important grew stronger.

He tried to open his eyes but they were sore too. He managed a couple of quick blinks, bright light blinding him momentarily. He let them flutter closed again watching the sunlight filter through his eyelids creating a red glow.

"How is he taking it doctor?" Came a familiar voice.

"Hard to say, he is coming around though, should know in a bit." Silas thought he recognized this voice as well. It was quiet again and he heard a soft beeping coming from somewhere above his head.

"Look at his skin though, it must be taking affect." The other voice said, this time he sounded nervous.

"Oh it most certainly is. We just don't know whether or not he will survive. That is the real experiment – time will tell."

"How soon will he recover? We don't have much more time, they are expecting him soon."

"Hawes, we do not have a time estimate, this is an experiment. Would you kindly stop asking me stupid questions and get back to your assignment?" The voice sounded harsh and the room went quiet again.

"Yes sir. We have an ambush scheduled for this afternoon – four exit points."

Something clicked in Silas's brain and he

realized he was listening to Franklin speak. He wondered what he meant by ambush.

The gruff voice interrupted his thoughts. "Good. Make sure you leave the small ones behind. They would be useless at this point."

"Absolutely sir, ping me if you need me." The familiar voice was talking quickly now and his voice shook.

"One more thing, if they get a look at you, fuzzy up their memory. We do not want any ugly speculation leaking out into the sector."

"Not a problem doctor. It will be done." After the door was shut and the footsteps had faded, Silas took the opportunity to open his eyes, curiosity overcoming his gut feeling that something dangerous was lurking in the room.

He focused his strength and cracked his eyes slightly. First he could see nothing but blinding light, then he turned his eyes away from the source of light letting them adjust.

He jumped when his eyes focused on a cruel looking man with bulging reddish-brown eyes and a rough salt and pepper beard. He was very stocky and his jowls shuddered a little when he saw that Silas had opened his eyes. He would have given everything he had to wake up to another face.

"How do you feel?" the doctor asked in a voice that suggested he did not really care. Silas fought to get his mouth open to speak.

"Um..." he croaked, and then his mouth slammed shut again. The doctor laughed a little.

"The fatigue will wear off soon, don't you worry." He inspected the monitors above Silas's head and marked notes on his clipboard.

"You know you really are doing much better than I had expected. Hawes was right in choosing you, you have the heart for it."

Silas just looked at him wishing he could speak so he could ask what was going on.

"Of course we are not finished, you need to be placed in our thermo-tank before the transformation is completed. And if you live through that, I think we have a winner."

The doctor grinned revealing a set of yellowish crooked teeth beneath his tomato-like nose.

"But now, I think it is time I show you the eyes. You won't be able to use them fully yet, but once the bonding has finished I think you will find them useful." The doctor pulled a small mirror from the cabinet and turned it toward Silas without hesitation. Silas waited for his eyes to focus on the image in the mirror. At first it looked just like him. Then he spotted the changes, subtle at first.

His skin was darker, an unnatural color of tan with a hint of gray. But as he looked at himself he noticed the biggest change – his eyes. They were exactly like the caged rat he had seen before. They were the same odd color of his skin and the pupils had long black swirling tentacles that reached around inside his iris, moving on their own.

He could not help but feel a little shocked at his reflection. The man staring back at him looked strangely alien. The hint of gray on his skin added to this effect. His eyes were fierce and rarely blinked. The muscles in his jaw looked tense. Somehow he appeared stronger; intimidating.

Silas was starting to feel uncomfortable staring at his own reflection. The doctor must have noticed his discomfort because he lowered the mirror, placing it on the bedside table face down.

The doctor was looking at him expectantly, his bulging eyes wide. But Silas just laid his head back onto the pillow. He was becoming tired fast and he wondered vaguely if something had gone wrong with the transformation after all. *Had the shock of what he had just seen been too much for his brain to absorb?* Whatever the reason, he did not have time to contemplate.

Suddenly his eyes began to close again and he let them go without a fight. The dream came quick, but it seemed to last forever. He was standing on the edge of a cliff looking down into a vast expanse of nothing below him. Waves of darkness floated in the empty space, and for a moment Silas thought he might fall.

He teetered on the edge, leaning back away from the cliff. Suddenly a hand grabbed his shoulder, spinning him around quickly. The face in front of him was terrifying. It was like his, but darker, the features full of malice.

The creature held him tightly with two strong hands that dug into his shoulders. They looked at each other for an immeasurable amount of time. The creatures red eyes boring into his with such ferocity that Silas wanted nothing more than to look away. But he couldn't, an unusual power seemed to be flowing from the creature keeping their eyes locked.

Suddenly, the creature lifted him from the ground leaving his feet dangling in the open air. One hand released his shoulder only to wind around Silas's throat. He gasped clawing at the hand around his neck, but the skin was hard as stone. Silas let out one last broken cough before the creature suddenly released him, sending him flying over the cliff into the darkness below.

The last thing he remembered of that dream was the cruel red eyes staring down at him, and a flash of yellow crooked teeth as smile broke out across the face of his enemy who was watching him die.

ELEVEN

Vadell was looking out of the passenger seat window of the aqua car when she spotted the tall building in the distance. The aqua car was a new product that her mother had been trying out for the factory. It ran exclusively on water, so naturally the company had deduced that it would be only suiting to call it aqua car.

Her mother was still on her mobile when she stopped the car in the parking area of the factory. Vadell waited impatiently, tapping her fingers against the tan vinyl interior. Giving up, she stepped out of the car and started walking toward the entrance.

It was a few minutes before her mother met her at the lifts. They shuffled in just as the doors slid shut. When they reached her mother's office floor, Vadell announced that she was going to explore a bit. Her mother nodded impatiently.

She was still on the phone. Vadell wandered the halls until she found two gaping holes in the wall, each lit with a dim green light. Above the two tunnels was a hologram that read:

Public Slides: Use with caution.

Each slide was a massive swirl of recycled material that ran to the first floor and basement. The architects of the building had decided that a slide would save valuable energy, and could be used for going down instead of the elevators.

The stairs were also an option, so the slides were rarely used. However, safety measures were still taken to prevent people from running into one another on the trip down.

Weight sensors, as well as motion sensors were built into the slides and connected to the computer system. Similar to an elevator, the slide had lights above the entrance to show that the slide was or was not in use.

Talking about the construction of the slides had been a favorite topic in her house for many weeks before and after it was built, so Vadell had no trouble using it.

She scooted awkwardly into one of the slides; the light began glowing green, signaling a safe time for travel. She let go of the handrails and shot down the slide so fast that her heart skipped. Though she had used the slide a couple of times before, it still took her by surprise.

Flying through the dark tunnel she kept her hands tight at her sides as she swirled around in circles. Suddenly she hit a sharp turn causing her stomach to leap and her hair to fly up in her face. The tunnel was extremely dark, she could barely see the outline of her feet in front of her.

Vadell spotted a light glowing far in the distance, then the tunnel opened up. She landed softly on a cushion and it took her a few minutes to realize where she was.

The basement area of the company was enormous. It was the place in which they stored all of the new equipment and test vehicles. Vadell looked around at the rows of cars, trucks, lifters, bots and even a hover car or two.

The larger, more important crafts were stored in the back. Vadell spotted a Hilo lift at the very back row behind an armored tank. Its massive blades were folded up, almost touching the forty-foot ceiling.

She approached the Hilo lift, carefully avoiding the front blades. The top blades were so dangerous that they had to be folded up in storage to protect people and other vehicles from accidentally bumping into them.

Vadell looked around for the storage bank. It would be the only way to sneak on without being noticed immediately. Finally, she spotted a black door, one small handhold on the side was protruding slightly from the metal.

Vadell crawled under the side wing, taking extra care not to touch the craft. When she had reached the storage bank door she slid her backpack from her shoulder.

Lync had been sure to give her all the necessary supplies. Luckily, Lync was an ambitious collector of tools. Vadell never even bothered to ask her how she had got them.

After rummaging through the tools in the backpack for a few minutes, she found the small black box. Extracting it quickly, she placed the scrambler on the ground beside the back tire of the Hilo lift, and then flipped the small red switch with her pinkie finger.

A quiet buzzing filled the air and Vadell smiled to herself. The scrambler was a tool made to confuse any vehicle security system, and they were extremely illegal. If she was caught using one she would be sentenced to imprisonment, regardless of the fact that she was only a teenager. The scrambler allowed her to touch the Hilo lift without setting off the security alarm.

So she opened the storage bank as quietly as she could. Too many vibrations would alert one of the other security systems nearby where the scrambler could not reach.

The door slid open and Vadell crouched down to see inside. It was big, bigger than she thought. She and Lync would fit easily, even when it was loaded with RT equipment. Vadell had crawled halfway into the compartment when she heard the elevator ping. She quickly closed the storage bank and flung the bag over her shoulder – barely remembering to pick up the scrambler.

The elevator doors began to open as Vadell threw herself under a worktable, slamming her shoulder against one of the metal legs. She bit her lip and clutched her shoulder, tears welling up in her eyes.

She held her breath when she heard footsteps walking toward her from the direction of the elevator. Vadell backed up under the worktable until she felt the cold metal touch her back.

She remained still as she watched a pair of black boots walk toward the lifts. She assumed it must be a guard. They patrolled the storage areas regularly, making sure that nobody had wondered down to the basement accidentally.

The boots walked to the work table opposite her and stopped for a moment. She could hear rustling and then the person turned and walked quickly back to the elevators. Vadell waited until she could no longer hear the elevator before she let out a deep breath.

Rubbing her aching shoulder, she crawled out from beneath the workstation and ran for the stairs. She did not want to get caught taking the lift up from the basement, so she ran up the stairs to the first floor before jumping on the elevator.

She was still breathing hard when she arrived on her mother's floor. As soon as she was safely inside, she collapsed onto one of the leather couches in the waiting area of the office.

When she had gained control of her breathing again, she got up and found her mother sitting behind her desk talking on her mobile as usual. It was a general rule that she not be interrupted when she was talking.

Vadell waited patiently on the other side of the desk. Her mother clicked off the phone and turned to face her. Her eyebrows rose slightly as she took in her daughter's appearance. Her knees were covered in dirt, sweat coated her face.

"Where have you been?" She snapped.

"Just exploring, I took the slide. And then the stairs..." which was mostly true; it wouldn't hurt to leave out the finer details.

"Mm, well, I am going down to the conference room to meet with some colleagues. But I'll be back in about an hour." Her mother picked up a black bag and threw her phone inside.

"Can I take the car? I'm going to have lunch with Lync." She kept her voice smooth and relaxed even though her insides were squirming. Her mother looked at her for a moment. Mothers always have a way of knowing when you are lying. But to Vadell's surprise, her mother relaxed and stood up, plucking the key from her desk.

"Be careful, it's just a test model." She handed the key to Vadell before turning and walking out. Vadell waited for the door to beep and then for the sound of the elevator before she opened the office door. She walked to the elevator down the hall and ran her finger in front of the sensor by the hologram that said *First Floor Lobby*.

The doors opened instantly and Vadell stepped

in. She was on the first floor before she could grab the handrails.

***

When she pulled up outside Lync's house the driveway was empty. Vadell waited for several minutes before Lync appeared at the doorway. She typed a number into the code slot on the door before jumping into the passenger side of the aqua car. She was wearing all black, her long brown hair pulled into a tight bun on the top of her head.

"What are you wearing?" Vadell asked.

"The question is what are *you* wearing?" Lync ran her eyes up and down Vadell's clothes disapprovingly.

"We aren't robbing a bank."

"The black blends in better with the cargo area – making it harder for them to spot us." Lync sighed and heaved the heavy bag from her lap to the floorboard where it landed with a thud.

Vadell could think of nothing else to say, she was too nervous. The whole plan seemed very dangerous and she wished they had more time to work out the details. But the letter Sam had sent seemed urgent. Both Vadell and Lync had thought that it would be better to act sooner rather than later.

Obviously going to earth would be the only way to find out the truth since the media was lying about everything and nobody else seemed trustworthy. Vadell thought that if they could manage to sneak onto a Hilo lift, then they could sneak back on again when they needed to travel back to NB1.

She parked the aqua car a few blocks from their destination. The two of them walked the rest of the way. When they made it to the landing pad there was a Hilo craft being readied for takeoff. Two Rescue Team members were standing together, heads bent down looking at something resembling a map.

The streets were still littered with trash from the last welcoming parade. A few teenagers were roaming the streets, standing outside buildings to trade illegal goods from earth.

Vadell followed Lync toward the fence that separated the landing pad from the rest of the city. The only people allowed inside were members of the Rescue Team and their commanders.

Lync pulled out a small black box and plugged

it into the code slot on the fence. It beeped quietly as Vadell watched the RT members walk around the craft, checking various parts before takeoff. Lync worked on the codes for a while before she poked Vadell's arm sharply.

"We're in." She whispered and motioned for Vadell to follow her.

The pair went through the gate and crossed the landing pad while the two RT members were busy with the other side of the craft. Lync crawled under the Hilo lift and Vadell followed her closely, making sure she was completely silent.

Then they waited, watching the two pairs of black boots circle the craft, one pair walked to the pilot side and climbed in, the other walked back to the hangar.

"NOW!" Said Lync urgently.

Vadell grabbed the storage bank door and pulled hard. It resisted for a moment before it finally fell open. Vadell crawled inside and Lync came next, throwing her black bag inside first. She was halfway in when they heard him.

"HALT!" The shock on Lync's face was a mirror of her own. They both froze and then Lync flew out of the storage bank and landed on the ground with a loud crack.

"AAAAH!" She cried out, grabbing her leg in pain. Vadell didn't know what to do. They were going to prison.

She grabbed Lync's bag and pulled it open looking for something, anything that she could use as a weapon. The RT officer hadn't noticed her yet, he was too busy trying to bind Lyncs hands. Vadell knew she had no choice but to attack him by surprise. If he spotted her, she was doomed.

She found the heavy black box that Lync had used for the codes on the fence and pulled it out, grabbing it tightly in her hands. She waited for the officer to turn his back to her, and when he did she flew out of the compartment.

Putting all her weight and strength in her hands, she slammed the black box down on the man's head. He cried out and fell to the ground, blood running down the side of his head. Vadell helped Lync to her feet and together they ran for the fence.

"THE BAG!" Yelled Lync.

Vadell turned, the bag was sitting inside the cargo hold, all the tools and supplies Lync had worked so hard to get. If it was discovered they would be in even more trouble.

"Run, I'll get the bag!" Vadell screamed at Lync who hesitated before turning to the fence.

Vadell ran as fast as she could to the Hilo lift. The man was still curled on the ground – he appeared unconscious. Vadell grabbed the bag and threw it over her shoulder. When she started to run for the fence she heard a shocked gasp behind her.

She glanced over her shoulder and saw two more Rescue Team officers running over to their fallen friend. One of them turned and began running after her.

She flew through the fence and closed it, locking it in place with a beep. She spotted Lync halfway up the street and Vadell ran hard to catch up with her, the heavy bag weighing her down.

It was only a few seconds later that she heard the beep of the fence being unlocked. She grabbed Lync's shirt, pulling her between a garden fence and a massive recycle bin. They both leaned against the cold metal waiting and hoping that the officer had not already spotted them.

She heard the sound of boots slapping the pavement and it was not long before they could hear the sound of labored breathing. Vadell held her breath and looked at Lync who was pale and shaking.

Lync's hands were trapped behind her back as she leaned against the smooth metal of the recycle bin. Vadell noticed that Lync's arm was bleeding from the fall out of the craft. Slowly she felt the muscles in her face relax as the sound of footsteps faded. Far in the distance she heard the roar of a patrol craft blasting to life.

TWELVE

Nothing could have prepared him for the pain he was feeling. His skin was on fire, burning to his skeleton. It felt like his raw nerves were exposed to the world, causing his eyes to water and his teeth to grind against each other. The doctor had failed to mention this part. He closed his eyes after a few minutes; it hurt too much to blink.

He was lying on a hard bed inside some kind of tank, completely encased in thick plastic, purple UV lights shone from every corner. Silas took deep breathes through his nose. Each time his lungs expanded his ribs ached and burned.

He could not see them, but he knew they were watching him closely. They would be waiting for something to go wrong, waiting for him to die. Suddenly, Silas could feel air flowing from somewhere above. It was icy cold and it felt amazing on his burning skin.

He peeled back his eyelids and stared above at the purple lights. Strangely they did not hurt his eyes. He caught a glimpse of something shiny. He tried focusing his eyes on it as it grew closer. Silas watched as the shiny object became clearer, it was moving toward his face, sharp and pointed. He panicked and pulled his arms against the metal cuffs that held his hands down.

His muscles screamed as he thrashed, the needle getting closer to his face every second. When it was only a few inches from his face, it slid down and aligned with his neck. He closed his eyes and scraped his fingers across the hard plastic.

Silas clenched his teeth when the cold needle pierced his neck. He waited for the pain to come, but he felt none. Perhaps something about the cold air had numbed his senses, he thought.

He wiggled his fingers experimentally, sending only faint shocks of pain up his arms. Silas watched the needle rise back up and soar through a tiny hatch at the top of the tank.

He was getting sleepy fast, and he let his eyes close without a fight. Silas did not want to fight anymore. A feeling of numbness washed over him, and Silas let himself relax into the cool darkness until there was nothing left. No dreams, no thoughts, only peaceful death.

But he was not dead; his headache was proof of that, the dead feel no pain. Of course he had no way of knowing that for certain, he had never died – *or had he?* Silas felt as though he had only been asleep for a minute. But as he lie there he could see sunlight through his eyelids and he knew it must be morning.

Silas opened his eyes and gasped. Everything was clear, unnaturally clear. It had to be a dream, his eyes had never seen anything this pure. He could see each ray of sunlight shining through the window; every speck of dust that reflected the sunlight, and every shadow cast by the speck itself.

The knock on the door echoed through his brain making him jump. He flexed his fingers – *at least I'm not sore anymore*, he thought.

The door cracked open, and the doctor walked in followed by two men wearing all black. Silas could not help but smile at their serious faces and matching gothic clothes. They were even wearing black sunglasses.

But a second later he was distracted by the doctor's face. He could see every pore, and every extra-long nose hair. It soon became too much and he looked away. Silas felt very pathetic not being able to look at someone because of their appearance, but everything was *too* clear. His head began aching again so he closed his eyes, resting his head on the pillow.

"A bit overwhelming isn't it?" The doctor's rough voice echoed through the room, making Silas's head pound.

"That headache will go away soon enough. When it does, we will have to leave." The doctor eased into the brown leather armchair by his bed making a crackling sound.

Silas opened his eyes again, but he did not look at the doctor. Instead, he kept his eyes on his hands; the odd color of his skin unusually prominent.

"What do you mean leave?" He asked, recognizing the difference in his voice immediately.

"We need you to help gather more soldiers. Since you were such a success, we can move on to others."

"No, we can't just take them. Even if they chose to do this it would be too dangerous."

Silas remembered how the man named Franklin had told him he could save the world. How he would be given extraordinary power to save his friends.

He felt extreme guilt as he thought about them. He had left them to fend for themselves while he risked his life on something that might not work.

"You didn't think you would be the *only one* did you?" Silas did not speak. Of course he already knew that, but he did not expect it to happen so quickly. "We have the power to create a new race; this is a breakthrough. The world changed the day we put you in that tank."

"And what happens when it goes wrong? What if the government gets your recipe, and builds its own army?"

Silas finally lifted his face to glare at the doctor, anger building up somewhere inside his stomach. His new senses revealed the quickest ways to kill the man in front of him. One hand around his neck would do it.

"The virus is safe, locked away in the deepest darkest part of this lab. No one will find it, I guarantee you." The doctor smirked, he seemed very proud of himself.

"You can't be sure of that." Silas tried to keep control of his temper; his hands automatically gripped the sides of the bed tight.

They stared at each other for a moment or two, neither of them surrendering. The doctor pulled a small hand-held device from his pocket and typed something quickly.

"The escorts will be here in three hours. They want you at sector four by nightfall." He slid the device back into his pocket and stood. "Don't even think about fighting me. You gave yourself to my lab. Now you belong to me, and to the rest of this team. You're a weapon, I cannot let you leave on your own."

"You can't do that! I didn't say you could take away my freedom." The doctor's fists tightened, his knuckles turning white.

"I wish you wouldn't make this hard for us. You don't realize how much we need you – how much the world needs you."

Silas raked his fingernails against the leather restraints that held him. "If you need me so badly, then allow me to choose."

The doctor did not speak, anger evident on his face as he pulled open the door and slipped out of the room, the two silent guards following.

THIRTEEN

Vadell dropped the heavy bag to the ground, and dug through it until she found the cutters. After freeing Lync from the binders, they took off running down the street, taking a back road behind a row of empty houses.

Most of the houses on the block were vacant. The houses near the landing pad were designed for the poorest families. After all, nobody wanted to live near the noisy takeoff area. Vadell and Lync ran down the alley until Lync grabbed her arm, pulling her to a stop by one of the houses in the center.

"We could hide inside the house." Lync said, her breath ragged from the run. She looked pale against her black shirt, a torn spot on the fabric revealed a bloody wound near her shoulder.

They looked at each other, and then Vadell picked up a small recycling bin and threw it at the window. It crashed through, leaving pieces of sharp glass hanging from the sill.

Vadell plucked off the biggest shards and then

helped Lync through the window. Once inside, they ran to the kitchen storage room and closed the door behind them.

Every house on NB1 had a thick metal storage room for kitchen goods. It also doubled as a safe room, should the owner ever need one. Unfortunately neither of them knew how to engage the lock-down feature.

"They can't detect us on radar in this room. The walls are too thick, even for their tools. One of the many things they didn't think about when building these places."

Lync grabbed a kitchen towel from the shelf and wrapped it around her arm while she spoke.

"They don't think people will even attempt to break the law here. Not after all they paid, and all they left behind to get here."

They waited as the sound of a roaring engine grew closer. It was so loud that it hurt Vadell's ears, then suddenly, the sound cut off.

Vadell looked at Lync who was staring straight at the door, waiting. It was quiet, nothing but the sound of their breathing pierced the air. Then a door somewhere in the house exploded – the Rescue Team had found their hiding spot.

Lync grabbed Vadell's arm and pulled open the door. They both knew there was no chance of getting away if they stayed inside. They ran through the house – Vadell dodged the dining room table, and spun into the master bedroom. She followed Lync, who was already crawling through the broken window.

Vadell was halfway through the window when she heard Lync scream. She looked down and saw Lync being restrained by a large man in a black armored suit.

Vadell turned to run back into the house, but instead she ran straight into a tall body, the impact sent her flying to the ground.

"Don't move." Said a voice, and she obeyed.

Vadell had no other choice but to surrender. The man grabbed her arm and pulled her off the ground with such force that she felt like her shoulder was pulled loose. He snapped her hands together and tied them shut with a set of binders.

When she emerged from the house, Vadell saw Lync sitting in the patrol craft, her head resting on the seat. The officer shoved her into the other side of the craft and slammed the door without saying a word.

She waited for the officer to walk away from the craft before she leaned over to peer through the thick glass divider at Lync. If it was not for the shallow rise and fall of her chest, Vadell would have thought Lync was dead. Her face was pale white, and her eyes were closed. She was slouching against the seat at an odd angle, her bruised face pressed against the leather interior of the craft.

Vadell's mind was racing and her stomach was doing back flips. There would be no way out once they were inside the prison, she knew that. Tears flooded her eyes as Sam's face appeared in her mind. She could never help him where she was going.

Any hope they had left of leaving NB1, and rescuing Sam, had ended when they attempted to board the Hilo craft. Vadell had felt it then, but she wanted so badly for the plan to work.

She laid her head back on the seat, and took a deep breath. She was busy trying her best not to have a meltdown when she heard it. Her head shot up and she looked around for the RT officers.

They were standing in front of the house talking – making calls on their devices. She looked at Lync who was still in the same exact spot as before, completely unconscious.

The craft was filled with a clicking sound; Vadell looked around frantically for the source. Then suddenly, her door cracked open and several things happened at once.

First, a man was grabbing her shoulder, and pulling her from the craft with such speed that she didn't even see his face. The patrol craft's alarm went off and the officers were running toward them at full speed.

Next thing she knew, she was being thrown into the passenger seat of a small craft. It looked similar to the Hilo craft, but much smaller, with massive blue jets beneath it.

She glanced around in confusion, looking out the window. She was already rising into the air. The Rescue Team was several feet below, leaping back into their patrol crafts and heading for the landing pad.

"Wait!" Vadell yelled and turned to find the pilot of the craft steering her away from her best friend.

Lync was still lying helpless in the back of the RT patrol craft. She would undoubtedly be sent to prison. When Vadell finally noticed the man driving, she was shocked. He was only a few years older than her, probably in his early twenties.

He was wearing grimy, torn clothing, and looked like he hadn't bathed in some time. She crawled across the seat and grabbed a handful of his dirty t-shirt.

"HEY! I said wait! My friend is down there!" He took one hand and pushed her back into the seat without looking at her. He did not speak after that, he only stared into the empty sky and steered the craft.

"Who are you!? I appreciate you saving me, but I have important things that I need to be doing. And if you don't mind you can just put me down someplace..."

"SHUT UP!" He said finally. He looked at her fiercely and she obeyed him.

His eyes had stunned her into silence. They were an odd brownish-gray color, and the pupils were dancing violently inside his eyes, swirling around like a tornado.

"I will tell you what you need to know, but first we have to find a hiding place. Let's hope that the RT is not already tracking us." His voice softened a little as he turned his head back toward the sky.

The lights of the city were turning off by the

time they flew past the border. Vadell watched the lights dying out one-by-one as they passed overhead. She began to wonder how they had not been caught, how nobody had seen them.

The rest of the flight was a silent one after her initial break-down. Vadell had so many questions, but she was afraid to ask him anything.

Something about his eyes held a certain power. She could see that he was not the kind of person you would want to annoy. Instead, she waited for him to speak first, but he never did. They had traveled far beyond the city, to the eastern edge where the world ended.

The ground below changed from cement, houses, and fake grass, to giant gaping holes of nothing. They were surrounded by protective boundaries made of laser fencing that nobody could pass through.

Some of the ground was made of basic extra light metal framing, and some of it held the newly formed ground made of mostly recycled materials. This was the foundation to support life on NB1. Vadell had seen this part of the world only once, when she had first arrived. The people on NB1 were not allowed to leave their respective cities. Once assigned, you were stuck there, forever.

He did not start lowering the craft until the ground beneath them was nothing but metal littered with the storage buildings that held work equipment.

They dove down causing the craft to shutter and switch into hover mode. They floated down into one of the massive holes between the metal support beams. Vadell was about to protest, but she felt it was best to keep quiet as the man began dodging pieces of metal and jagged spikes.

It was so dark that the only light for miles was the blue glow of the engines beneath them. They hovered down for several more feet before the man reached over and flipped a switch by the steering wheel, which caused a blast of bright light to shoot in front of them. It was so bright Vadell was sure that anyone flying above could see the glow of it coming from the depths where they traveled.

Vadell was starting to wonder if they would ever stop. They had gone so deep that she could no longer see the sky.

Finally, the craft slowed and almost stopped before they turned and went straight into one of the metal walls.

Vadell thought for a moment that they would crash, but the man pulled up on the steering wheel and they soared into an opening that was barely large enough for the craft. They flew for another few minutes until Vadell could see a faint glowing ahead. When they got closer she could see it, it looked like a small village built directly onto the metal support beams.

Lights glowed from the inside of the small canvas tents scattered across the ground. From above, the tents resembled a thousand stars twinkling in space.

FOURTEEN

"Focus." Silas stared at the lifeless mannequin breathing hard. Nothing happened.

"I can't do this." He whispered as he sank into the small plush chair. Franklin walked forward and sat down in front of him.

"I know you don't want to be here, but as long as you are forced to be here..."

"I know, I know, – I might as well learn something." Silas interrupted. The whole thing seemed pointless, though he tried hard to feel optimistic.

At least Franklin had managed to convince the doctor that he needed more time to adjust to his new abilities. The downside, of course, would be that he was sealed into a small padded room from which he was never allowed to leave.

The only life he saw came with Franklin's visits. The doctor had allowed him training, and agreed that Franklin was the perfect person to prepare him for what he assumed would be something dangerous. These training sessions would happen twice a week, for five weeks. At the end of that time, he would have to leave for sector four – willingly or not.

"The hardest part is, we aren't sure exactly how to go about training you." Franklin adjusted his tie. "We can only speculate about what you are capable of. You're the first real success we've had."

Silas just glared at the mannequin. The first week had been the hardest. Adjusting to what he could see was hard enough, but he could also hear everything. He could smell his dinner being prepared across the building once a day through the sea of thick metal that separated each room from the other.

A loud ping interrupted his thoughts, and Silas looked up to see Franklin standing.

"I guess time's up for today." Franklin said quickly. Silas couldn't help but notice something odd about the way he had spoken.

"I know you don't want to go, but I think it would be wise, if you would... *cooperate*." Franklin grinned for what seemed like a fraction of a second, before turning and walking through the wall.

Silas sat confused about what Franklin had said, or more importantly, *the way he had said it.* He looked down at his oddly colored hands; a thick metal ring was clamped firmly around his right wrist. The small light on the side of the band blinked red slowly. Wristbands were attached to everyone at the lab, each with a different color light according to rank.

Prisoners were attached a red light, which made it impossible to leave the door-less rooms constructed for special prisoners like Silas. People of higher rank, such as Franklin, were allowed a green light. This gave them free range to come and go from any room – apart from the doctor's private study. The doctor himself had no wristband at all. Silas had yet to figure out how he was able to walk through the walls as he pleased.

The last week of his stay had made Silas increasingly annoyed at Franklin, who had decided to avoid any questions about his previous behavior. Silas still wondered about the hint that Franklin had given him, if it was a hint at all. It could only mean that Franklin knew something about the trip to sector four that he did not. Silas was staring at the clean white ceiling when he heard someone approach the wall directly outside his room. The familiar sound of raspy, labored breathing made him sit up on his bed. Watching and waiting, he heard the voice before the face appeared.

"Well, I do not approve you lying around all day." Silas felt his muscles tense, his fingers curling into fists. "We leave in twenty- four hours and yet..." The old man paused walking forward, leaning his hip against the padded white armchair. "You have not even begun to explore your abilities. I'm disappointed."

The doctor shook his head, prompting his jowls to tremble. Silas stood then, barely containing his anger.

"What am I supposed to do?" He glared at the doctor who just looked at him curiously. "You keep me in this prison all day."

The doctor grinned flashing his gnarled teeth.

"We have provided you training. Yet, you resist even that."

Silas felt his fingertips digging sharply into his palm.

"If you want me to practice, master – I will practice." He felt the grin spread across his face as he let the red-hot anger flood from his eyes. He was sure the doctor noticed the change because he took a tiny step back. Silas could hear the doctor's heart quicken and he smiled wider.

In an instant, so quick that he was only a blur, Silas flew across the room at the doctor. His hands had barely touched the doctor's thick throat when he felt excruciating pain shoot through his arm. Silas fell to the floor trying desperately to force himself back up again, but the pain continued, and his eyes blurred. His ears filled with a ringing that caused his head to pound.

Finally, his vision cleared and he saw the doctor standing over him. His face a mixture of emotions; fear, anger, and a few others that Silas could not recognize. Suddenly, the doctor smiled.

"I'm impressed. The speed is truly amazing." He ran his watery, bloodshot eyes across Silas's face.

"Don't worry about the shock, it will wear off soon."

Silas felt that he was missing something important, but his brain was fuzzy. He looked up at the doctor in a haze of confusion.

"We had to test your abilities, and this seemed the best way. I do hope we can get past this." He spoke with a certain fake sincerity that made Silas wish he had succeeded with his attack.

The doctor extended his hand to Silas who waited, debating his next move. Then, suddenly inspiration struck him. Silas reached out and took the doctors rough wrinkled hand in his inhuman one.

"Thank you." Silas said smiling. He felt extremely confident that this was the only way to go. The doctor looked confused for a moment, and then he smiled.

"I knew you would see the truth." He hoisted Silas to his feet with some effort and then squeezed his hand tightly. "So we are on the same page then?"

"Absolutely sir." Silas lied.

FIFTEEN

Silas had decided that the best way to get what he wanted was to cooperate. That was what Franklin meant, he needed to gain trust. Then once he was in the air, he would put his plan to action.

The doctor was thoroughly pleased when Silas said that he would be going willingly to the sector. The morning of his departure, everything was going according to plan.

Of course they still did not trust him enough to let him on the craft unrestrained, so his hands were bound, and his eyes covered. Silas still did not know of the power his eyes held – and he definitely did not want to risk trying them out now, when he was unsure of the outcome.

All he knew was what the doctor had told him; He was dangerous, he was a weapon. The doctor stayed behind at the lab, but sent Franklin with them as a babysitter.

Silas felt a ping of frustration, he had hoped that Franklin would stay behind as well. He liked Franklin, at least more than he liked the rest of them – and Silas did not want to hurt him.

Silas had a steady plan for breaking free, but he felt the *after* part was still a bit ambiguous.

He needed to find supporters, people that could help him stop the doctor before he went too far. He also needed to get the remaining survivors onto the new planet without being caught.

The Hilo craft burst to life, its giant blades spinning them into the dust-colored sky. Silas sat perfectly still in his seat, waiting for the precise moment when he would put his plan into action. The pilot was busy steering the Hilo in the direction of sector four. Silas could feel Franklin's eyes on him, waiting for something to happen.

The rest of the crew seemed preoccupied by their various tasks. Fortunately, so was the guard placed there to monitor him. Silas ran his fingers across the smooth plastic wrapped around his wrists. Binders, they were impossible to escape unless you held the passkey.

Even though his eyes were covered, Silas could sense the people around him. Whenever a pair of eyes fell on him, he knew almost instantly who they belonged to. He was not sure if the lab knew about his new skill, but he had no intention of telling them. Even though he was considered part of their team, something about him made everyone uneasy. He could hear their nervous hearts beating – his personal guards heart sloshed hyper-actively as he eyed him.

Silas focused his mind away from stray thoughts, and concentrated on the guard. He could hear his breathing, hear the sound of the sweat running down his cheek. He allowed himself to be absorbed into the guard, feeling the exhaustion of the day, the burn in his eyes as he tried not to blink.

Then, Silas tried his new skill for the first time. Instead of feeling what the guard felt, he turned it around, forcing his emotions on the guard. He threw his mind into one goal, unlocking the binders. He heard the guard shuffle in his seat, then the sound of a compartment opening.

He tried to ignore what was going on, and focus on the key. Silas curled his hands into fists, clenching his teeth hard he thought about how desperately he wanted the key.

Suddenly, he felt hands on his arms pulling him sideways and the beep as the binders fell from his wrists and landed on the seat.

He released his mind from the guard, and quickly ripped the mask from his eyes. The world burst to life in front of him, shapes and textures so beautiful he had to force himself to concentrate on his task. He had not seen the outside world for weeks, and it was overwhelming.

Silas moved quickly, turning to face the guard before the crew noticed his escape. He stared straight into the guards gray, bloodshot eyes and felt the power radiating from his own.

The guard started shaking, and Silas focused harder, pushing the energy out of his eyes. The guard twisted once in the seat and then slumped down onto the leather, completely unconscious.

Silas had no time to think about anything; flying from the seat he grabbed Franklin's shoulder, throwing him into the back of the Hilo craft. The pilot turned to look at him, his shocked face had turned white.

The pilot reached desperately for his hand-held device, but Silas beat him to it. Silas crunched the device in his hands and threw it behind him where Franklin was trying to crawl to his feet.

"Land now!" Silas said, and the pilot looked at him for a moment, considering. He was braver than Silas had thought. "We are going down one way or the other. Keep in mind I can take a rough landing better than you can." This seemed to motivate the pilot as he pushed buttons, sending waves of flashing lights across the inside of the Hilo craft.

They were headed straight for a small clearing of dead grass, but the trees were too thick, the gigantic blades of the Hilo craft could not fit. The pilot lowered the craft anyway. As the trees got closer, Silas clutched the back of the pilot's seat, and prepared for the crash – but the crash did not come.

The Hilo craft was lowering right onto the trees. With the sound of metal slicing wood, Silas watched as the blades turned the trees to mulch. As soon as the craft touched down, Silas grabbed the pilot, turning the man's face toward his own.

He looked him in the eyes feeling the power building up inside him. The man quivered and slouched in his hands, unconscious. Silas threw the pilot from the craft where he landed with a thud on the hard ground. Unsure of how long the effects would last, Silas worked quickly.

He turned to Franklin who was lying on the floor, face white and exhausted. Silas unfolded his hand and held it out to Franklin who looked at him suspiciously. After a second or two, he finally extended his hand, and Silas lifted him off the ground.

"Come with me." Silas said, he had always liked Franklin, and it seemed that Franklin was never bothered by breaking the rules. Franklin just looked at him and then he smiled, his eyes crinkling at the corners.

"You know, I almost wish I could." He folded back his sleeve and held out his arm. "You see this?" He gestured to the pink and white scar on his arm.

"What is it?"

"They won't let me leave. They know where I am at all times, and they will come for me. They know we have stopped moving."

Silas felt a strange mixture of emotions looking at the man in front of him, but most of all he felt pity. That was why Franklin had been so keen to break the rules – he was not one of them. He was forced to be at the lab, forced to play by the doctor's rules just as Silas was.

"Why didn't they tag me?"

"Oh they tried." Franklin ran his fingers along the thin pink line on his arm. "Your blood is too powerful, it destroyed the chip."

Franklin smiled at him again. "Maybe we will see each other again, someday. I feel like a change is coming. I feel like maybe, the end is not really the end we all thought it was, but something greater." It was quiet for a moment. Silas could feel it too, the change in the air. Something big was coming.

Franklin jumped out of the sliding door and landed on the ground beside the unconscious pilot. Silas smiled a little to himself when he closed the door to the craft. The plan had worked. He was on his way, though he did not know where. All he knew was that he could not sit around and let everyone die.

He was going to make things right again. The Hilo craft shot into the air as Silas switched on the day camouflage.

He had never flown a craft as big as the Hilo, but his new senses made everything easier. He rose to meet the sky, voyaging into the endless land ahead of him.

SIXTEEN

When the doors to the craft opened, hundreds of people were standing around the edges of the landing pad. Some peered curiously at her through the crowd, others looked suspicious – some disapproving.

Most of the people were dirty, their clothes torn. It appeared that none of them had eaten much, and they all looked tired. Vadell's kidnapper took her arm and led her toward one large tent in the middle of the small underground village. Dim lamps lit the walkway ahead of them.

The man did not talk to her as he pulled her into the tent, closing it tight behind them. Two people were waiting inside, standing in the center of the dimly-lit room. The tent was huge, much larger than it appeared on the outside. Its immense white canvas ceiling stretched on forever. Pillows were stacked around in circles, surrounded by old-fashioned candles and torches.

"Ah, welcome back. And who do you have with you?" A tall, thin woman with long red hair spoke. She was standing next to a shorter, slightly balding man, whose beady eyes scanned them both.

The woman did the same, she looked once over Vadell and then back to the man still clutching her arm. She looked pleased.

The man beside Vadell flopped down onto a pillow, and Vadell thought it best to do the same. She was tired from the long flight, and it felt strange leaving him to be the only one sitting. The two others followed, sitting so close to one another that their knees touched.

She jumped at the sound of his voice, she had not heard him speak since they left. His voice was powerful, the kind of voice that made you pay attention. She turned her head to face him. His odd skin looked almost beautiful in the dim light of the flickering candles.

"This is," he paused looking at the two strangers quickly. "Vadell." The two looked at him, and then at her. The woman looked mildly curious as she let her eyes linger on Vadell. The man, however, seemed to be in shock.

"How did you find her?" The man blurted out. His hands shuffled together nervously as he glanced back and forth between the odd looking man and Vadell.

"It wasn't that difficult, she was making quite a scene in the center of the big city. RT officers were everywhere."

"Wait!" Vadell interrupted their flow of conversation. "How do you know my name?" She never remembered telling him her name. And why had the other two recognized it?

"You didn't tell her?" Said the tall woman, her green, cat-like eyes squinting, and her eyebrows coming down to meet in a sharp point.

"I didn't want the cities sound grid to hear me – you know that." They looked at each other for a few seconds.

"Well, looks like you have some explaining to do." She ran her eyes over the two of them again and then stood, gesturing for the short man to follow.

"We better go, let you two get more acquainted." She bowed low to Vadell and then at the odd man.

"I'm so sorry to confuse you, Vadell. You must be very curious as to why you are here. I'm sure my dear friend will fill you in. Good night, child." She bowed again and flew out of the room before

Vadell could respond. They sat quietly for a moment and then the man turned to her.

"I guess we should start at the beginning." He ran a hand through his messy black hair. "My name is Silas Grissom. The people here were brought from earth." Vadell could not speak for a moment. So many people from earth; she wondered if one of them had been friends with Sam, or carried the letter between them.

"But how?" She said quietly. Silas looked at one of the torches, the flickering light reflecting off his swirling, inhuman eyes.

"It wasn't easy, I can tell you that much."

"What does this have to do with me?"

She had wanted to ask him this for so long, but she was too afraid of him. Now he seemed different, more relaxed, more controlled.

When she had first seen him he looked dangerous, deadly even, and now he looked almost peaceful.

"Because someone who helped me back on earth needed help, and I owed him."

"What do you mean?"

"He said he had only one request, that I find you, and bring you here – fill you in on what is happening." Silas's eyes flickered to her; she watched the swirling pupils dance around like tall grass in a high wind. She could not believe what he was saying, and at the same time she was thrilled by it.

"Sam." She said. He nodded once slowly.

"He said that I had to bring you back when I made the next trip, said it was extremely important."

She stared at him, amazed, everything had worked out like magic. She felt a ping of worry when she remembered her friend who had been captured. It seemed like years had gone by as she pictured Lync lying on the cold dirty ground in a metal prison cell. The thought sent chills along her skin.

"Lync, my friend, I left her behind. You didn't give me the chance to save her." Vadell felt unexpectedly angry at Silas for leaving Lync behind and taking her.

Who was he anyway that he could just abduct people when he felt like it?

"I didn't have a choice. Do you think they would have just sat there and watched while I busted her out? I didn't even know she was in the car! I didn't even know she existed!"

"You wouldn't let me say anything! How could I tell you?" She exploded at him.

"You obviously don't understand. Did you not see the mess you made? They would have caught us, and I didn't want to make a mess of them in public." He looked at her, his eyes swirling faster than before. She felt her rage cool, turning into an icy chill.

"I am going back for her." she looked at him sternly, trying to sound confident about her decision. "Sam wouldn't leave her behind."

"Well, I'm sorry but Sam is not here." Silas resounded. Vadell turned her head away from him, she did not want to look at him, she wanted to feel angry not frightened.

Sam had put her in a dangerous position. Of course he could not have known that Lync would be in danger. Or that he was making it harder on her by having someone come for her when she was perfectly capable. Vadell felt that Silas was not the kind of guy to give up easily, or be talked into something very quickly, so she pushed the subject no more. When he realized her defeat he stood, and she followed him.

"I will fill you in on everything in the morning, but for now it's late, we need to rest." He threw her a stack of pillows from beside a table. "Goodnight."

Silas marched out, leaving her alone in the empty tent. She spread the pillows on the ground and lie down looking up at the shadows of the dancing flames on the ceiling. It was a beautiful sight, but she felt strangely sad.

It was a weird thing to be lying there with people she didn't know. All of them hiding from the people who had taken everything away – hiding right under the enemy's noses.

And then her mind drifted between worrying about Lync, and worrying about Sam. Wondering what they were both doing, if they were safe, if she would see them again. She could only hope for the best. Only hope that they would all make it out of this alive.

SEVENTEEN

He had been flying for hours, and the landscape remained the same. Flat ground with the occasional patch of dead grass was all that could be seen apart from a line of trees far in the distance. No matter how long he flew, the trees remained the same size.

Silas was beginning to question his sanity. For the first time since he broke into the lab, he felt the cold stab of fear. He didn't know where he was going, or what he was looking for. He had nothing to hold onto apart from the hope that he would find someone out here.

Luckily, the lab had used a Hilo craft to carry him to sector four. This meant that he could fly for a very long time without having to refuel. Unfortunately the engine was prone to overheating, and because of this he would be forced to stop every few hours – whether he found a suitable landing spot or not.

The reason for this problem was the earth itself. Its crumbling atmosphere allowed the blazing sun to burn the surface, killing most of the plants and animals. The Hilo could only withstand so much of the earth's heat before giving up.

Silas's mind was racing from one problem to the next. If he was forced to land he would have to stay in the Hilo craft, and away from the burning sun. Silas did not feel like putting his new body to the test while stranded in the middle of nowhere.

After another hour of flying, the craft could take no more. It spluttered and jumped along the orange sky until he spotted one single tree coming up from the dirt, its limbs bare and cracked. The craft shuttered as he prepared to land near the tree. The blades began to spin faster and faster, sending a spray of sand flying through the air.

The Hilo touched down lightly and the engine shut off, heaving one last exhausted breath before going silent. Silas waited for the dust to settle before stepping out to look around. He could still see the silhouetted trees in the distance, but they appeared no closer than before.

Silas raised his hand to block the sun from his sensitive eyes, but saw nothing apart from the empty landscape around him. However, the light smell of smoke on the breeze told him he was not alone.

The RT had used excuses for the fires, saying that they were purely natural; a terrible side-effect of a dying planet. They were trying to make people believe that they were doing something good by rescuing the innocent from these disasters.

But Silas knew better than to believe the lies. He had seen firsthand how the government had taken the lives of those they thought undesirable, or useless to the new world.

Silas wasted no time searching the area for anything useful. But the scorching sun had left little alive. He knew that only the night could bring relief, and so he waited inside the craft – waited for the sun to lower itself behind the profile of the unreachable forest.

Suddenly, the ground shook, Silas sat up alertly looking around for the source. *I must have fallen asleep.*

At first he could see nothing but the dimly lit expanse around the craft. Then came the fire, a blazing sphere of flames flying straight for him. He panicked, tearing out of the craft he ran to the line of trees, which had turned black from the sun sinking behind them.

The sound of steel on steel slamming into one another caused him to fall forward. Holding his ears, he desperately tried to debar the screeching sound that penetrated his skull. Finally, the sound dissipated, and he looked up at the wreck that was his only transportation.

The Hilo was completely crushed by the monstrous piece of flaming metal that had fallen from the sky. Silas stared at it in shock; he needed that craft more than anything. It was his only shelter from the sun, and his only way out of the wilderness.

Another tremor made him jump. Looking up at the sky he saw what looked like stars falling from space. The closer they got, the more he noticed what they really were – flaming debris from some unknown disaster.

Fire was everywhere, an unavoidable mass that would destroy anything in its path. He knew there would be nothing he could do but run and hope that he could dodge the destruction.

So he ran, fast and hard. The first one hit, spraying him with dirt and fire. Suddenly, another fiery ball slammed into the ground in front of him with such force that he was blown back, skidding painfully into the sand.

Before he could stand, another fireball soared from the sky striking him hard in the chest. He felt one moment of searing pain as the heavy metal crushed his ribcage, and then everything disappeared into the eventide.

EIGHTEEN

His scream of pain echoed around him as he woke, his head slamming into something hard and cold. Silas spent one disoriented moment trying to figure out where he was, and then he noticed he was sitting in the Hilo craft. It was perfectly unharmed, apart from the substantial crack in the window created by his head.

He sat up quickly, feeling his ribs for anything out of place. *Nothing.* Silas sat there confused for some time, wondering what could be happening to him. Never had his dreams been so real, it was as if he could feel the pain he felt in his dream, even in his waking moments.

Silas glanced through the cracked window at the rising sun, he had been asleep much longer than he thought. He was about to start the engine again, when something moved along the tree line in front of him.

It took him a moment for his eyes to adjust before he saw it. A person was kneeling on the ground near one of the dead trees. It was a boy, no older than seventeen, and he was completely unaware of Silas. When the boy looked up at the Hilo craft, he seemed mesmerized by it, his eyes were wide and his mouth hung open. Silas was certain the boy could not see him inside the Hilo, since even Silas's sensitive eyes could barely see the boy's expression from such a distance.

Suddenly, the boy turned and ran back into the trees with such speed that Silas felt a little impressed. Silas quickly started the craft and pulled back on the steering wheel, sending the Hilo soaring into the air.

He flew toward the line of trees, pushing the craft for all it had and then some. Still it seemed like years passed before he was finally upon his objective.

The forest resembled a graveyard with hundreds of dead trees sticking up at odd angles, bark twisted and falling off. He found a small patch of dead grass to land on, and lowered the craft into the trees. Silas had two motivations for finding the mysterious boy.

Firstly, he was determined to figure out what anyone would be doing in a deserted forest so far from civilization. And secondly, Silas was desperate to find someone; another living thing that shared his goal of surviving a doomed planet.

Silas landed the craft softly and cut off the engine. When the sound of the roaring machine died, Silas held his breath, listening carefully for footsteps or breathing.

The door slid open and he jumped out landing unobtrusively on his toes. Silas stayed frozen to the spot, listening, watching, and using all of his senses to absorb the information around him.

But there was no sign of life anywhere. It was like the boy had vanished. Silas trusted his senses, and he knew that if the boy was hiding somewhere in the forest, he would be able to feel his presence.

But there was nothing, not a single whip of wind blew through the gnarled branches – but Silas was determined, he knew that somebody was out there, and he was going to find them.

He returned to the Hilo craft, and grabbed a bag, stuffing it with anything he might need for a trip on foot. Taking the craft would be useless, he needed to feel the environment – taste the wind for any sign of life.

Silas threw the backpack onto his shoulder and began walking through the forest. It was a blistering day as usual, and Silas felt his energy drain. He had not eaten in two days, and the strain of his new body was wearing him down. It was not the physical strain that hurt him, but the mental. It seemed as though he burned three times the energy using his extraordinary mental abilities, and his escape had left him exhausted.

The forest itself offered no relief from the deadly sun. The bare limbs blocked little sunlight, allowing most of the rays to fall on his unprotected skin. But he was strong, much stronger than any human, and as much as he tried to avoid thinking about it, he was definitely *not* human.

Two hours passed slowly under the hot sun. Silas could hear his own pained breathing as he used the last of his energy reserves. Suddenly, he heard a soft sound coming from someplace deep in the forest. It was the sound of dripping water, far off, but unmistakable. Silas pushed forward through the dead trees, tearing off limbs as he went.

He could not believe his luck, as he grew closer the sound became more distinct. It was the sound of water falling onto rocks. Silas focused in, trying to pinpoint the direction it was coming from. *Drip, drip, drip...* He put his hands on the trees to either side of him, feeling the earth, the connection

BRITTNEY STEWART

between the trees and the ground, the ground and the *cave*. He could see it now in his mind – a cave, small and dark, buried in dead grass and surrounded by trees. The water inside dripped slowly from somewhere above. The harder he focused, the more detailed the image became. His mind was straining to stay conscious as he let go of the image.

The soft dripping had turned into a very audible smacking sound which sent sound waves through the ground and into the trees, vibrating his arms.

He dropped his hands; ignoring his exhaustion, Silas ran through the trees at full speed. He was getting closer, the smell of water in the air. He could almost taste it – cool, clear, and fresh.

He ran until he could see the glint of sun shining on a black rock. Finally, he arrived at the cave, but he approached it cautiously, waiting for any sign of movement. *Drip, drip, drip…*

Silas crouched down by a tree and watched the cave. He could see the entrance slightly obscured by the bare trees around it. He heard nothing but the steady drip of water. There was not a single indication that anything was living there. Deciding it was safe; Silas stood and slowly approached the cave. Reaching into his back pocket, Silas pulled out a small old fashioned hunting knife that he had found in the Hilo craft. It was minuscule, but it was all he needed.

When Silas reached the cave entrance he peered into the darkness, his eyes adjusting quickly. He could see immense stalagmites crawling up toward the ceiling of the cave. It was much larger inside than he had expected, it even appeared to go underground.

As Silas took his first step into the cave, a blast of cool air hit him hard in the face. He welcomed the respite, and continued deeper into the darkness.

Once inside, he could see it all clearly – the walls were moist, and water dripped from the ceiling. It was the first time in years that he had seen fresh water flow so freely in the natural world. This water did not drip from a faucet, but appeared on its own.

Silas found a small cleft in the rock, and scooped a handful of water, drinking it hastily – cooling his dry throat. He walked on for what felt like hours. He was surprised by the depth of the cave, which seemed unending. It was dark, but his uncommon eyes could see just fine – gathering light from every source including the sunlight that bounced from rock to rock. The cave reminded him of when he was younger, when there was still some green left in the forest. There was never much, but he loved to explore it. Now it was all gone. The very few forests left were bare and dry.

Silas had not seen a green leaf in years. Nothing would grow after most of the world began turning into desert. The animals could not survive the temperature, and neither could the plants. One after another the world's inhabitants simply died off like a cascading set of dominoes. Silas feared the same fate for humanity.

The new world was supposed to change everything. They could let the planet die, and then move to another one. This was to ensure that mankind lived on forever. But Silas hated this idea – he hated that the government interfered where it simply should not.

The old world, the new world, and even his mutation were all examples of this problem. He felt a sudden pull in his stomach, a stab of sadness when he remembered why he had done it all.

The whole thing was for his friends, for his family. But he could not find them, and maybe he never would. He had escaped the doctor, but now he was lost, alone, and chasing someone he only thought he saw – someone who might not even exist.

Silas stopped walking, and dropped to the cave floor, resting his head on the cold stone wall. No matter how much he had been changed through his mutation, that part of him remained; the part that wanted to make sure everyone made it out alive.

But it was *impossible,* there was no way he could do it on his own, but even if he did have friends to help him, the job was too big. Too many people would be left behind, even if he managed to rescue some.

And the real rescuers would continue to torch the world, aiding the blazing sun until nothing remained but a flat expanse of dust and ash. Silas closed his eyes and let the agony seep in. Then he heard it, the swooshing sound of air deep in the cave. He held his breath and listened. It was quiet and then another blast of air. He stood up and ran toward the source leaving his bag behind.

Silas felt a magnetic pull toward the sound, it forced him to run even faster. He did not simply want to discover the source of the sound, but he *needed* to. It felt like the answers to his problems were right there in front of him, waiting to be snatched. Silas ran until he felt like floating, his breath steady, and his eyes never blinking.

For a fraction of a second, Silas thought he caught a glimpse of something that resembled a waterfall ahead, a wall of glistening clear liquid. He tried to stop, but it was too late, his body slammed into the translucent wall, pain shaking him from the impact.

And then he was floating – floating through a dark tunnel of clear wavy liquid. It was like being underwater, although he was completely dry.

He began to float faster, and faster down the dark tunnel. His stomach churned as he was thrown around unable to gain control. Silas closed his eyes and waited. A sickening thought occurred to him; *maybe he would never leave this place, maybe he had died and this was his eternity.* But he must have been wrong because he felt a tug on his ribcage. He was slowing down.

Then he could see a light, dim, and glowing steady in the distance. The sudden intensity made his eyes hurt, he tried desperately to readjust. His eyes were becoming blurry, he blinked but it was only getting worse as he traveled farther into the light. Black splotches formed in his vision.

Silas laid his head back, letting his eyes close halfway. *Just a small nap would do* – he thought to himself as the outline of a person appeared in front of him.

NINETEEN

In his dream, Silas was charging down a field of dust. Fire burned all around him as he ran, gritting his teeth, and holding a spear tightly in his fist.

Staring back at him from across the murky field was a colossal pair of bulging red eyes. The eyes were surrounded by thousands of smaller, lighter, colored eyes.

Silas could see no individual outlined in the dust storm around them, the falling ash landed on his eyelashes, further obscuring his eyesight. Silas raised his spear and tightened his muscles, ready for the moment when the two sides of battle would unite.

There was a roar from both sides as they collided into a flash of color, sending a blast of dust and blood into the heavens. Silas had never seen anything like it. Something felt out of place. He worried briefly that he had forgotten something of great importance.

Suddenly, he could see it; the eyes were getting

closer, burning red-hot from beneath a midnight hood. The cloaked figure moved toward him, and Silas raised his spear. With every ounce of strength he had, Silas threw the spear into the grimy darkness where only the red eyes could be seen.

But Silas was too slow. The figure snapped the spear in two with one stroke of its magnificent black-bladed sword. Silas reached for his dagger, but he was too late. He felt the sword pierce his shoulder, the pain sending him to his knees. Just as the figure stood over him, preparing the last deadly strike, everything changed.

Colors swirled, and images mixed to form new ones. Silas heard other voices, people talking in sharp whispers around his head. He tried to focus his eyes, but all he saw was a blurred outlines in front of him

"Can you hear me dear?" Came a sweet girly voice from someplace nearby. "Oh please wake up..." she said again. Silas jumped when he felt a tug on his shoulder where the cloaked figure had stabbed him. "Oh be careful will you! He isn't made of stone." The girly voice said in a harsher tone.

"I think I know what I'm doing, Sage." A new

voice said petulantly. Silas felt his arm tug again, causing his teeth grind against each other.

"I don't appreciate your tone!" The female voice said again.

"Well, you can just go somewhere else, and leave me and my tone in peace!" Silas felt himself smile at the argument.

When his brain had gathered itself back to reality, Silas began to remember more of the dream, and more importantly, the happening at the cave. He opened his eyes quickly and sat up causing the room to erupt into gasps.

"Now we don't mean you any harm mister!" A short woman in the corner of the room spoke. She was holding an old towel in her hands, twisting it around her small, thin fingers.

"He's fine, Sage! Aren't you?" The man beside him smacked his shoulder, causing Silas to jump at the sudden pain.

"Oh sorry!" He apologized before holding out his hand. "My name is Ben, and this is my wife Sage." He paused and waited for Silas to shake his hand. "We're refugees."

Silas nodded as they shook hands. "How did you find this place?" Silas asked, his head throbbing.

"Purely an accident. Right, Sage?"

"Yes, Ben was getting water from the cave when he fell in." She smiled at him.

Sage was a short, thin, middle-aged woman. She had thick, curly, brown hair that she wore short. Ben was much taller and also thin, with a scraggly beard and balding brown hair.

"I never had such a shock in all my life. Took me a while to find my way out." Ben chuckled as he stood. Walking around the bed, he began picking up pieces of gauze.

"But, once I found the exit portal it was easy enough to get in and out. Of course it makes you a tad dizzy your first go round. And your second..."

"Is it normal to uh, pass out?" Silas felt a little ashamed.

"Well some people do, some don't. I would say it's pretty common." Silas watched him clean up the area around the bed. When he finished, Ben turned to him and looked curiously at his eyes for a moment.

"What is your name, boy?"

Silas flinched and considered lying, but he knew somehow they already suspected who he was.

He could tell by the way they stared at him. They were asking a question they already knew the answer to.

"Silas, my name is Silas." The two looked at each other. Ben's face screamed – *I told you so* – Sage just looked at him, her eyes wide.

"What?" Silas asked. The couple looked from one another, to Silas, and back again in awe.

"We know who you are." Sage said quietly. "We saw you on the news."

Silas felt a dull pain in his stomach. They had already started searching for him. But, of course, it made perfect sense – they would be using all of the resources they had to find him. He was the lab's most important weapon, and they would do anything to get him back. He could only hope that he was alone when they did find him. Any spares would be killed, or maybe even turned into the lab for experimentation. He could not be the cause of any more death.

Silas must have looked as bad as he felt, because Sage spoke up. "Don't you worry, we wouldn't dare tell them you're here."

"Of course not!" Ben agreed. "We don't believe in that sort of thing. In fact, we don't believe in anything when it comes to the government anymore. Bunch of liars..." Sage nodded proudly at her husband. Silas's mind drifted to his lost friends. Those he had left behind when he broke into the lab. It felt like years had passed since then. But the guilt he felt for them was still fresh in his mind. He didn't know where they were, if they had been killed, if they had left him for the new planet.

Even though Silas wanted his friends safely on NB1, part of him was hoping that they would not leave without him. He wanted so badly to believe that he meant that much to somebody.

Later, when Silas had been bandaged, bathed and given fresh clothing, the three of them walked silently down a dark tunnel. The walls were stone, and old fashioned torches had been attached to the walls, their warmth soaking his skin – the feeling was pleasant after his bath in the cold stream.

From what he had seen so far, they had nearly everything they needed, including water and shelter. But he was not sure how they managed to find food until they passed an immense opening in the cave.

Silas peeked in and saw a vast open space. Grass unlike anything he had seen in its rich color covered the ground. There were people, about twenty of them, working with tools – planting, and watering. Various types of plant life shot up from the ground, tall, short, and in every color imaginable.

These people knew how to obtain what they needed for survival. They were safe, hidden away from the rest of the world, deep in the cave. Of course, Silas knew that once the planet was gone, even the cave could not keep them safe.

But the most confusing part to Silas was the sunshine. He could see it, patches of blue sky peeking through small window-like holes in the side of the cave, a hundred feet above them. But he knew well enough that they were buried deep beneath the earth.

When he fell into the abyss, he fell down, not up. The color of the sky was another thing that troubled him. Silas had never seen a sky so blue not even when he was young.

He remembered the days, running through the partially deserted streets, the sky a dull, gray-brown.

Once in a while he would see it, a peek of blue; it would happen so quickly, that once he blinked, it would be gone. Something about this place was magical, and he felt it. Something filled the air that made him know hope for the first time in months.

He had refrained from asking any more questions until he was settled, and everyone was comfortable with his presence. He was after all, not the average person.

Silas wanted to gain their trust, to earn it if he had to. He would need these people, and they would need him when the war began – which he knew it inevitably would.

After much walking, Silas and his two companions arrived in yet another gigantic chamber. Light flooded the room from holes similar to those in the harvest chamber.

The windows seemed much larger, however, in this room. Silas thought he noticed the slight glare of the sun created only by glass.

Silas stared inquisitively at every detail, his newly improved eyes absorbing the scene. He was marveling at the blue sky far above when someone spoke.

"Well look here!"

Silas turned to see a short, chubby man with long, curly blond hair, and a short beard standing in front of him. He reached out a plump hand to Silas who took it with caution. The man had a strong presence, and Silas could see that he was a leader.

"My name is Vik Zar, Welcome to our home!"

Vik shook his hand hard and then released him. The man gestured toward a long homemade table that stretched the length of the cavern.

Silas followed Ben, Sage, and Vik to the table where the four of them took seats at the end. Silas noticed that the chairs had been crafted from wood with great detail. He wondered idly where the materials had come from.

"Thank you for allowing me to stay here. I didn't mean to fall in on you." Sage laughed at Silas's pathetic joke, and patted his arm. The act was so motherly that it reminded him of his own parents, and this made his head throb a little.

"Oh, nonsense! We are absolutely delighted that you are here!" Vik said, puffing out his chest and rocking ever so slightly in his chair. He really did seem delighted.

"We assured him he was safe here. He is so nice, such a good kid." Sage said as she continued patting his arm.

"Oh of course he is! You, my boy, are the one we have waited, and hoped for." Vik looked at Silas, his expression becoming more serious.

"I've been searching for you, too. You don't realize how surprising it was to fall in here." Silas looked up at the ceiling again and watched a puffy, white thing float by the window. The white mass resembled smoke, but it was different, pure, and beautiful.

"Well, we are so, so happy to have you. We prepared a room for you in one of our biggest chambers. I hope it is satisfactory." Silas sighed at the wonderful gift, he felt unworthy of it.

"I really don't think that's necessary." Silas said, shrugging. Vik seemed insulted by the very idea that the gift may not be accepted.

"Nonsense, you will be sleeping in the chamber we prepared for you. Why let all that work go to waste?" Silas looked at Vik without speaking, silently accepting his offer.

"Fantastic! Let's go have the tour now, before dinner. They will need a little more time preparing for the feast."

"Feast!?" Silas was shocked; surely it would not be for him.

"Of course! We have been praying for you to come here." Vik beamed and leaned forward in his seat.

"The feast is for me!?" Silas stood and the three before him watched with wide eyes. Vik laughed, the sound echoing through the cavern.

"Yes, it's for you! Who else would it be for?" He chuckled again and rocked in his seat, his curly hair bouncing around his face.

Silas thought of a thousand replies, but only managed a mumble. Vik stood unexpectedly and began walking away from them down another tunnel.

Vik stopped and turned to them. Ben and Sage were still sitting. "Well, aren't you coming?" He said and then turned away; Silas could see his curls bouncing with laughter as he walked. Ben stood then, pulling Sage up by the arm. She reached out her free hand and took Silas's.

"Come on dear, you are going to love this place." She looked at him with kind, soft eyes. He felt a fondness for her that he could not explain – it felt as though she was family.

The tour had been a long one. Silas had seen so much of the caves, yet Vik said there would be more. The cavern felt like miles of winding stone and openings that formed rooms, some small, some large, but all amazing, each with high windows revealing the pale sky.

There were dozens of individual chambers sealed off from the rest of the cave. These were private quarters for permanent residents, which were typically shared by families. It was not until he reached his own private room that Silas got to see the inside of these dwellings.

The space was huge, not unlike the other rooms of the cave. It was much smaller than the harvest room, or the dining hall, however – but quite a sizable space for one person.

The walls were made up of the same stone as the rest of the cave, a dark brown marble streaked with lighter colors. The windows were located high in the ceiling. The floor was also stone, with large rug sprawled in the middle of it. On the rug sat a wooden bed, it appeared old, but comfortable.

"We will call for you when dinner is ready." Vik said as he gestured for Ben and Sage to go ahead of him. They looked at Silas and then smiled at each other before leaving the long entry hall of his room.

"Thanks, really, I don't deserve all of this..."

BRITTNEY STEWART

Silas ran a hand through his hair. There was no way to thank Vik for letting him stay so comfortably when he was no more than a stranger.

"Psht! You deserve every bit. We all know who you are. We all know that you are here for a reason." Silas nodded once, and then Vik turned to walk down the tunnel.

Silas waited until Vik's shadow vanished. When he could no longer hear or smell any sign of a person in the tunnel, Silas turned and dove onto the antique wooden bed. He landed face-first in a mound of maroon blankets, causing the old boards to groan.

Silas lie there for several minutes thinking of nothing but the comfortable bed, and then it hit him. *Could they be in the cave too?* The people he had left behind on the day he set out to find and steal the secret weapon? They would know he was alive, know what had happened to him. They would at least know that he had been changed, and what he had become.

The news would change the story of course, as they did with everything. He sat up, then leaped from the bed.

He started to run for the doorway, and then he stopped. It would do him no good to get lost in the tunnels and not make it to his own feast, he was overreacting. Silas thought it through, if they were with him in the cave, they would come to the feast. He would find them then.

Silas took a deep breath, and explored the room a bit before returning to his bed. It seemed like he had only been lying there a few minutes when he heard footsteps coming down the tunnel to his room. He sat up and waited. He could smell her, the flowery sent floating in the air between them. Sage peeked around the corner.

"Hello!" She smiled at him and then entered the room. She was wearing a bright green, handmade dress, and leather sandals. "The feast is about to begin. Vik told me to bring you these." She handed him a folded stack of clothing.

"What are these for?" Silas said as he took them from her.

"They are gifts from the women of the caves. We made them for you." She smiled broadly.

A surprised thank you was all he managed to get out. Silas couldn't understand why they thought he was so important, why they treated him like royalty.

"Vik said you should wear them to the feast.

It would make everyone so happy." She patted his shoulder and then walked toward the doorway. "See you in a few minutes?"

"Yes. Thanks again, for everything." Silas said, and he meant it.

He had only been with these people for a few hours at most, and yet they had given him more than anyone ever had. Silas felt at home, an emotion that was foreign to him.

Silas finished dressing, and then looked into the old, rustic mirror propped against the cave wall. The shirt was black with long sleeves; it was adorned with silver thread sewn in intricate patterns around the neck and wrists.

The pants were much the same, with silver patterns flowing down the sides. Silas felt odd dressing up for dinner. He had wore blue jeans and t-shirts for his entire existence.

By the time he reached the end of the entrance hall to his room, Vik was already waiting for him. He too was wearing a long sleeved shirt and pants with the same silver threading.

The patterns were different, however, and the color of the fabric was a deep blue. He looked Silas up and down, and then nodded his approval.

"The women here are fantastic weavers. It is really quite amazing to observe." Vik turned and started walking quickly away.

"How long have you lived here?" Silas asked when he caught up with him.

"Twelve years." Silas felt his eyes widen. He wondered how long the place had been there.

"Wow. This place really is incredible."

"Oh, it's more than that! You haven't even seen half of it yet!" Vik chuckled, slowing his pace as they neared the entrance to the dining hall.

"Here we are, everyone is waiting for you."

The room was packed with people, the walls lined with them, and every chair was taken. Servers walked around the room wearing glittery costumes that flickered in time with the candlelight of the tables.

Silas was hit with an overwhelming amount of information. The sights, smells, and sounds all mixed together and formed one loud buzz. His head throbbed as the noise became more prominent.

"This way." Vik said, heading for the end of the table where two reserved seats sat empty. Silas took the seat beside an old woman in a purple dress and matching hat made entirely of flowers.

She nodded at him once, and then turned her nose up and away from him. Silas shrugged off her rudeness and turned to Vik, who was pouring a glass of something from an old bottle.

"Attention! Attention!" He called and every head turned toward him at once. Some still whispered as they stared, but Vik waited until they were done before giving his speech.

"Today is a great day for our colony. Not only have we been fortunate enough to find safety in our refuge these past few years, but this man, who has promised to save the world, is here with us now." The room erupted into applause.

"He is the only one of his kind, so we should treat him with great respect. He is different from us, but I ask every one of you to treat him as family, because he is part of our family now."

The crowd was silent as they watched Vik. Most of them looked delighted, while others eyed Silas suspiciously.

"And so now, we shall enjoy this feast we have worked so hard for. Let's eat!" Instantly the room filled with the buzz of talk. People were reaching for food as they stared at him when they thought he couldn't see.

Silas examined the plate in front of him. He had never seen food like this, it was homegrown and homemade. Everything he had back home was instant or dehydrated, apart from the small tomato plant he kept in his house. The plant was extremely rare, a gift from his grandfather who knew everything about plant life.

After he ate a bowl of some strange vegetarian stew, the next course came. A short, plump woman wearing the same glittering robes as the other servers approached him. She smiled widely as she took his bowl.

After a minute of watching the others, and listening to the nearest conversation, the next course appeared in front of him. It was a kind of wrap, made completely of vegetables. The food was delicious and by the last of seven courses, Silas thought his stomach would burst.

Then Vik turned to him. "You never did tell us where you were from."

Silas struggled in his head for a moment, wondering if it would be safe to tell the truth. Not all of the sectors were friends... "Um..." He started, but Vik took over.

"You have to understand. I have been wondering for some time, you see, the news doesn't tell us. Perhaps they don't know..." Silas lowered his head to his plate looking at the last course, a light salad – untouched.

"Well, I grew up in sector nine, but my father moved us to sector seven, when I was a teenager."

Vik patted his shoulder. "That is terrible, just terrible!"

Silas didn't understand what Vik meant by that. Silas opened his mouth to speak, but closed it again. Vik looked at him curiously, and then to the lady next to him. She looked back with a worried expression.

"Don't you know?" Vik whispered.

"Know what?" Feeling completely confused but sensing something bad, the muscles in his face tensed.

Vik sighed before continuing. The lady next to him was watching Silas closely now. "They lost sectors three, fourteen, and seven in the fires..." They were all studying him now as he clenched his fists on the white linen tablecloth.

It felt like someone had slammed his head against one of the cave walls. The throbbing in his skull made him lean forward, placing his face in his hands. Silas felt a hand on his shoulder, the loud chatter in the room had died down to a faint whisper.

Vik spoke then. "I think it is time for our guest to turn in. Those of you who feel up for cleaning may stay behind and help the servers. I'm sure they would appreciate it. As for the rest of you, goodnight."

There was the sound of a chair scooting, and then Silas raised his head. Vik was standing, and after some hesitation the others followed.

The crowd began talking again; many of them watched Silas from the corner of their eyes. Silas did not care anymore, he felt numb thinking about sector seven and his lost friends. His head throbbed again as he followed Vik and the others from the room.

Finally, when he and Vik were alone, Silas pulled Vik into the shadows – his eyes watering from the pain in his head, and from the tragedy that stabbed at his heart.

"How many died?" He whispered to Vik, who was looking at him with a worried expression. He paused, as if deciding exactly what to say.

"The broadcast said... Well, nobody was rescued." Silas felt a sinking sensation as despair flowed down into his stomach. He let go of Vik's arm, and without saying goodbye, escaped down the hallway into darkness.

When he arrived in his room, Silas collapsed on his bed. He wished more than anything that he could stop his mind from racing. He knew that most of the others had left the sector. But what about those that stayed – those that were supposed to wait behind until Silas had secured a solid plan.

On the bright side, the news broadcasts were rarely factual. Silas wondered what had really happened. Vik said that nobody had been rescued, but that didn't mean they had not survived.

When his mind had relaxed some, Silas let himself drift into an uneasy sleep. Flashes of horrifying images flew before his mind, and every few minutes he would wake up gasping.

He opened his eyes to see the moon shining through one small window near the ceiling. He had never seen a moon like this before – it was stunning, brilliantly white, and shining luminously.

The moon he had known was a dull yellow, and so often covered by thick, brown clouds, that he almost never saw it fully. He spent the rest of the night looking up at the sky, marveling at the stunning glow.

When the moon finally disappeared, and the stars faded, Silas knew that dawn was coming. The sky lightened to a purple-orange color, and Silas lie there watching until it turned blue – rays of light flowing through the small windows. Grudgingly, he pulled himself out of bed, feeling the weight of his new body for the first time.

He was exhausted without sleep, which was a negative side effect of his new body. He used much more energy than any normal person.

Once he had dressed in a fresh pair of clothes, Silas walked through the dimly lit tunnels, toward the dining hall.

Food would help his lack of energy, he thought, so when he saw Vik and a few others eating breakfast, he did not hesitate to join them.

When Vik saw him approaching, he turned to the two women with him and said something. They immediately got up and left the room.

"Good morning, how was your first night here?" Vik said in a friendly tone.

"Um, really good." Silas lied as he sat down in

BRITTNEY STEWART

the empty chair next to Vik.

"Listen," Vik started, looking a little concerned. "I should have been more aware of my actions last night. It was wrong of me to bring that up in public." He folded his hands together on the table as he spoke.

"It's nothing really; I just wasn't prepared to hear..."

"Well, that is behind us now. If you can forgive me, that is..." Vik still looked apprehensive.

"Of course, it wasn't your fault." Silas said, taking a small sip of water from the glass in front of him.

After the servers brought him as much breakfast as he could hold, Vik said his goodbyes and floated off down another tunnel. Silas sat alone at the long dining table, thinking. It was still early and many of the residents were asleep.

After some time, Silas heard the sound of voices coming from various parts of the cave and knew that the hall would soon be full of people in search of breakfast.

Not wanting to be stuck in the crowd again, he stood up and grabbed a piece of bread from the table before heading into a long, dark tunnel. The caves were confusing, everything looked so similar. He followed the tunnel for a long time, not meeting a single soul.

Silas found another vast opening in the cavern. He was blinded by the brightness of the room after being in the dark tunnel. This room was different from the others, with brightly colored walls, and rows of handmade benches.

Part of the wall across from him was decorated with hundreds of paintings. These were not expensive old paintings, like those he saw in museums when he was young – these were unmistakably the work of children. Distorted houses and figures waived from their two-dimensional world.

After a while he moved on, continuing up the passage until he felt the floor vibrating. The tremors made his ears buzz, but he kept moving forward until he could see dim light in the distance. He could hear the sound of something drilling, or hammering into rock as he moved curiously forward.

It was a while before he reached the end of the tunnel. The light was coming from several lamps that were hanging along the passage. Silas peered around the corner sneakily.

There were several men holding torches, in front of them were even more men, all using clubs and axes to bore into the rock. It looked like they were getting nowhere as they pounded the rock face.

Silas saw small pebbles falling from the cave as the men hammered incessantly. Suddenly, Silas heard a faint growl behind him, and before he could turn he was flying through the air.

TWENTY

Silas slammed into the stone wall and fell to the floor. His shoulder pounded – he was surprised more harm had not been dealt by the blow. He was fortunate that his new body could handle more damage. The downside of this was, unfortunately, a bad temper. Silas pulled himself to his feet, regarding the darkness.

He spotted movement ahead, his muscles tensing automatically, readying himself for battle. He ran down the tunnel at full speed. Rounding the corner he managed to skid to a halt right before he smashed into a giant furry body.

Silas looked up to see an angry face looking back through a pair of bulky tusks. The face was pig-like, but the eyes were human. The creature raised its massive hands to swing, four inch claws slashing the air.

Silas instinctively ducked, and avoided the blow sending the creature into the wall. The ground shook from the impact as the creature hissed in pain. Silas had been so busy he had not even notice the men standing down the tunnel, watching and hooting with excitement. He was about to run for the tunnel, when the creature surprised him with another swing.

Silas dodged again, but this time one of the claws hit his face, squirting blood across the cave floor. Silas grabbed the creature's furry brown arm as it tried to prepare another blow. He pulled hard, heaving the creature into the stone. Only then did he notice the metal chain dangling from the creature's thick neck. It was tethered to something, guarding the tunnel against intruders like some bizarre guard dog.

The men down the tunnel were keeping their distance, but clearly enjoying the show. The creature stood shakily and lunged at him again. Silas decided to make a run for it. He had experienced all he wanted of the creature.

Bolting down the dark tunnel, he ran for several minutes, the beast hulking along behind him on all fours, shaking the ground with its weight. The tunnel was getting darker, *I must be getting deeper in the cave*, he thought.

Silas looked behind him at the hairy figure slumping along and growling madly. It was surprisingly fast for its size. Suddenly, there was a choking sound, and one extremely loud thud, so loud that Silas stopped running. Turning he saw a ball of fur on the floor. The creature stood and turned to him, pulling hard on its chain, but the chain would not budge.

They looked at each other for a minute. Silas could see in the monster's eyes that it would cause him no more trouble tonight. Slowly, the massive beast turned and made its way back down the dark tunnel, leaving Silas completely alone in the darkness.

He took off again, running for the only exit he knew, the dining hall. After several minutes of jogging – which was easy for him to maintain – he trotted out into the hall.

A few people were still sitting around enjoying breakfast when he emerged, breathing heavily, sweat dripping down his face. The room erupted in gasps. Silas froze, confused, and then he remembered his forehead.

He ran his fingers over his skull causing blood to run into his eyes. Turning quickly, Silas ran down the familiar tunnel to the hospital wing. As he ran he peered into rooms, and listened to the shocked gasps of people he passed in the tunnel. After nearly missing it, he wheeled into the hospital wing, which was mercifully empty. Silas sat down on one of the wobbly old beds for a few seconds, waiting for his breath to return to normal. Then Ben appeared in the doorway.

"My lord! What have you done to yourself!? Old Mrs. Webster told me about your condition and I hurried here right away." He was grabbing supplies from the shelves and loading them into a basket. Then finally he sat down in the wooden chair beside the bed and looked him over with interest.

"I sort of ran into something in the southern tunnels." Silas said, keeping his tone light.

"What do you mean you ran into something? Looks like you were mauled."

Ben pulled out some thick, green-colored cream from the basket and placed it on the bedside table.

"Well, I think I found a part of the tunnel that maybe I shouldn't have..." Silas said slowly as Ben scrubbed his forehead clean.

"What!" Ben shouted, "You don't mean... um when you say Southern..." Ben stuttered, and Silas was a little confused. "You weren't in the school tunnel were you?" He finally said.

Silas thought about this for a moment, trying

to make sense of the name. Then he remembered the room with the paintings, and the colorful walls. Of course, it was the school – Silas felt like banging his head on one of the cave walls. Ben sighed at the expression on Silas's face, which must have given him away.

"Nobody is allowed in that tunnel 'cept on on school days when the teachers take their students there. And even then it is only permissible for a select few... how did you manage to get that far down the tunnel?"

"I don't know... I just walked until I ran into some filthy looking creature..."

"Oh, no." Ben interrupted him, his face turning white.

"*Oh no?* What does, *oh no* mean?" Silas felt his stomach tangle at the look on Ben's face.

"It's just, I mean it sounds like you've..." He stuttered again, and then he looked down. "What did you see down there?" Ben whispered looking up at Silas.

"Well, I was watching some workers break through the cave wall, and then I got knocked around by this big hairy creature." Ben gasped.

"What!" Silas shouted trying to get an answer.

Ben blinked.

"Sounds like you met the Narkil." Ben said leaning toward him. "Very few have seen it and lived."

Silas had never heard of such a thing, and he had certainly never seen one before the confrontation.

"What are they doing down there? Isn't it dangerous to have a creature like that so close to the children?"

"Well they *are* dangerous, but Vik thinks they are a necessary risk." Ben shook his head as he threw the bloody rag into a bucket.

"What is so important that they need those for protection?" Silas asked. Ben started to look white again.

"We don't know, but it's important – something big." Ben looked over his shoulder as if someone was watching him. Then he turned back to look at his work. "I think we will need something a little stronger than anti-bacterial lotion for that. Narkils have very nasty bacteria on their claws." He ran over to a nearby cabinet and plucked out a small bottle of purple liquid.

Settling back into his seat he carefully uncorked

the bottle, pouring a little on a damp cloth. Ben rubbed the purple-stained rag onto Silas's wounded head. The sensation was amazing, instantly the pain went away, replaced by a pleasant tingle.

"Good, it's already healing." He corked the bottle and carefully placed it in the basket along with the unused green ointment. "Listen, I just want you to be careful around here, don't let anyone know what happened. I mean no *details.*"

Silas considered this for a moment before jumping off the bed. "OK, but you better tell Sage. She will be worried."

Ben rolled his eyes. "Yeah..."

He heaved the basket into his arms and Silas helped him put the contents away. Silas spent the rest of the day with Ben, hoping to get more information about the tunnel miners, but Ben would not share what he knew.

When the light finally faded in the dining hall, Silas retreated to his private quarters. He was tempted to explore the cave, but his last trek through the Southern tunnels had ended less than desirable. He hoped that nobody knew of his scrap with the Narkil, although news seemed to travel fast in his new home. Silas was also looking for any sign of a friend, anyone from sector seven that might have taken refuge in the caves. But he had no way of finding them, unless he bumped into them accidentally. After all, he had not seen the boy from the forest.

Silas doubted Vik would know where every single refugee was from, especially if they did not wish to share the information. The population of the cave was more than he had originally thought. The odds of seeing one of his lost friends at random was slim.

Then a plan struck him. He could wait for everyone to sleep, and then have the caves to himself. This seemed like the best plan since he would not have to worry about running into people, and appearing more suspicious than he already did.

He was quiet enough with his new body not to wake anyone, and if anyone was already awake he would know it. Silas changed out of his bloodstained shirt and into a clean cotton t-shirt. As he waited for the sun to set, Silas wondered what the digging was about.

He was sure they did not need to expand the caves. There was plenty of room, more than enough for the refugees. But he had never seen any other entrances to the cave. The odd sky outside made him wonder what could be out there. Maybe that was the reason they were digging. They were trying to find another exit out into the unknown.

But could it really be unknown? It would probably lead to another dead forest, somewhere the RT hadn't got to yet. But Silas could not explain the sky to himself. That was the flaw in his theory. It was too perfect, nothing like the sky he knew – blue and alien like the deepest parts of the sea.

TWENTY-ONE

When the sound of laughing and talking had died, Silas waited for the edge of the lustrous white moon to peek over the edge of his windowsill. Something about the moon in all of its colossal glory made him feel alive. He was truly aware of his surroundings, and for the first time, in control of his new senses.

It was completely silent in the dark passageway, and his presence did nothing to change the atmosphere. Silas moved without a sound down the empty tunnel toward the dining hall, where all the tunnels met.

The dining hall was immense and empty. It looked eerie, even bigger than usual. Something about the light from the moon gave it a majestic gleam that Silas had never seen. He looked at the entries to the different tunnels and spotted the one he had wondered down earlier in the day.

It was the third away from the biggest dining table. But he was not going down that one again, at least not yet. He moved swiftly toward one of the two tunnels he had not explored, and entered the darkness. Vik had showed him many parts of the cave, but he had left three tunnels at the far end alone, saying he would save it for another day.

Silas moved quickly, but silently down the shadowy tunnel. He felt his eyes gather the reflecting light of the moon, enhancing his night vision. It was a very tall tunnel, twisting and turning around many corners. Silas was careful to keep his senses sharp, listening for any sound that would alert him if something were lurking in the darkness ahead of him.

It felt like he could almost hear the air itself in the silence – a slight buzzing in his ears, that made him think he might have gone deaf. Then he heard something else. It sounded like a vibration, but it was distinct, not like the one he heard before. It was coming from someplace further in the blackness.

His curiosity pushed him forward, and around yet another corner, the buzzing growing louder with every step. Finally, he came to a small, dark room. It was round and not a single torch could be seen inside.

The moon was shining in, brightening his vision, making it look almost like day. The room was empty, but he could hear the buzzing vibrations so loud that he worried it might wake someone. Silas searched the room with his senses, looking for anything that might cause the noise. Then he saw movement in the corner of eye.

Silas jerked his head around as he noticed something silver shoot through the sky like lightning. He could do nothing but watch as the little sliver speck zoomed through the air. It stopped suddenly, and flew slowly toward him.

Fluttering before his eyes was a tiny creature. It looked like a little monkey, but hairless and silvery-blue. Its wings sparkled as it hovered in front of his face, observing him with knowing eyes. Silas saw his own hand move up and he wondered vaguely how it had gotten there.

He felt like he had no control over his own actions, but strangely, it did not worry him. In fact, Silas felt completely at ease. He watched the little creature land on his palm. The silvery wings stopped fluttering at once, but the buzzing still continued.

Suddenly, Silas realized it was not the wings that caused the buzz; it was the tiny heartbeat of the creature. Silas watched it for a minute as the creature settled into his palm comfortably. He was not sure what to do, he was afraid that it would fly away. Then, the lamp in the corner flicked on causing him to jump. The little creature flew up toward the ceiling. After his eyes adjusted, Silas could see a figure walking toward him in the dim light.

To his shock, it was Vik who stood before him dressed in a bathrobe, clutching an old shabby book in his thick hands.

"I'm sorry I just..." Silas began, but Vik raised a hand to stop him.

"No trouble here. I heard about the incident earlier. Of course I don't blame you for being a little curious." He nodded toward Silas's face. "I'm guessing you met our Narkil." Silas brought his hand to his face mechanically.

"Yeah, Ben patched me up."

"Lucky for that. They are very nasty, Narkils." He moved to a chair behind a large desk in the center of the room and sat down. Silas followed him, sitting on the opposite side in the small wooden chair.

"Well, now that you know about that part of the cave, I might as well tell you..." He leaned forward resting his arms on the desk. "We are trying to dig our way out." Silas was not surprised; he had assumed that much already.

"You can't tell any of the others, they think that we sealed off the exits to keep out intruders. Especially when we don't know what is living in the other world yet." Vik said casually.

"*Other world?*" Silas said and Vik seemed a little confused.

"Of course, obviously that is not the same world out there," he gestured to the window above his head, "that we knew before we came here. It's a very magical thing this cave."

To Silas it made sense, and then it did not. He wasn't sure how it could work. But then again he had seen so much in his recent journey that he would have thought impossible before.

"You mean you have never left the cave?" Silas said, and Vik laughed.

"Oh believe me, we have tried. When we first arrived here the cave was empty, but there was evidence that people lived here before, long ago."

"How do you know that?"

Vik pointed over his head again at one of the windows, a perfect circle. "The windows were here, long before us. And the most curious thing of all

– the barriers."

Silas raised his eyebrows as Vik continued. "The windows have a glass-like material in them, just like any ordinary window, but they are completely unbreakable."

"Sounds like whoever built this place was pretty advanced."

"Yes, but the question is, why did they leave?" Both men pondered this in silence as the little creature twirled in the air over their heads.

"We found this little guy caged inside the cavern." He held out his hand and the small silvery creature landed there. Vik looked at it for a moment smiling. "We found the Narkil also, and a few dead specimens. That is how Ben was able to study them."

"Where did they come from?" Silas asked. The creature looked at him over its tiny shoulder.

"We think they must have come from outside. Which means, whoever lived here was trying to keep something more dangerous out."

Silas looked at the windows again, the moonlight was still streaming in. "Then why do you want to open it up again, if whoever lived here worked so hard to keep that area separate?"

Vik considered this for a moment, and then he picked up a wrinkly photograph from his desk drawer. He handed it to Silas who ran his eyes across the image quickly.

"This is from the fires." He spoke, and Vik nodded.

"That was taken a few months ago. One of the refugees brought it with them." He leaned forward again on his desk looking seriously at Silas. "Don't you see? The world is dying. If we can't get these people onto the new planet..." He shook his head and leaned back.

"You're thinking that whatever is out there is going to be better than our world?"

Vik looked up, his eyes full of desperation. "It *has* to be, we have no other choice."

"Why are you telling me all of this?" Silas felt suspicious of Vik for the first time since he had arrived.

"Because, we need your help. We have been hoping that someone like you would come..."

"Someone like me?" Silas interrupted.

"We knew that the government had something planned, that they had some kind of weapon to finish us off. At first we didn't know it would be a person, but when we saw you on the news..."

"How? When did you see me?"

"The sectors have been broadcasting secretly across the world. They are trying to challenge the new government." Vik rocked a little in his chair, nervously. "They are bragging about you being the big weapon. They want to use you to take on the new government." Silas sat straighter in his chair, anger building up inside him.

"They can't honestly believe that one man can do that." Vik laughed suddenly, making Silas jump.

"Of course not!" He laughed again, but then stopped once he saw the look on Silas's face. "What I mean is, you were the reason this all happened. They used you, they changed you. And now they are making more of you."

"But they can't, nobody would volunteer, would they?"

Vik smiled a little, but did not laugh. "They don't need volunteers, not now."

"What do you mean?"

"They started drafting people – they're creating an army." Silas felt his stomach burn with anger.

"So how exactly do you plan to stop them?"

Silas said through gritted teeth.

"Well...that is still under construction. We may not need to stop them, if we can reach the new world in time." He stood up then, and Silas did the same. The little creature had taken to buzzing around their heads in a wide circle as they walked toward the doorway.

"Tomorrow, I will show you the rest of the caves, if you are up for it."

"Absolutely." Silas said before shaking Vik's hand and leaving back through the tunnel.

He returned to his room down the very long passage, but he took it at a run. He was able to run for hours if he was not utilizing his extraordinary mental abilities. And Silas liked running, it was easier and much quicker than walking. If he could refrain from using any extra talents, he would be much stronger if a battle was necessary.

TWENTY-TWO

The next morning Vik wasted no time retrieving Silas for the tour. Silas was barely dressed when Vik came charging in, handing over a wrinkled paper map. Silas flattened out the folded creases and studied the map closely.

Vik had prepared them a veggie wrap for breakfast, so they ate as they walked through the tunnel Silas had roamed the previous night. They passed Vik's personal quarters and continued on to a place marked on the map as the training area.

When they arrived in the large circular opening, Silas was amazed at the astonishing space before him. Most of the equipment was made of wood, many having intricate details.

"Have a look around I need to speak with Zuma." Vik said before heading off toward a tall, thin, black-haired man who sat in the corner, polishing a small dagger.

Silas roamed the stack of weapons with his eyes wide. He stared in amazement at a wall lined with old-fashioned swords and knives – most of which were no longer in use. The government had better ways of keeping control over the population, so they banned and discarded all weapons that were used in physical combat. Silas was certain that everything in the room around him was illegal.

A massive axe hung from a chain on the cave wall. Silas lifted it off and swung it through the air. It was heavy, but it felt perfect in his hands.

He threw it up toward the ceiling where it twirled three times before he caught it again. Every time he slashed the air, it was as if the wind itself screamed for his mercy. The blade was amazingly sharp, Silas was sure it would be a danger to even his strong skin.

He placed the axe back onto the chain and moved on. Another wall was set with an array of weapons he had never seen – such as two pieces of wood held together by a small chain in the middle.

A weapon with a metal handle sat on the shelf next to him. It too had a chain dangling from the end. But instead of another piece of wood or metal, a massive steel ball hung there, covered in deadly spikes.

The handle of this weapon was covered in what Silas recognized immediately as dried blood.

He was busy slamming a spike-covered club into a wooden dummy when Vik returned with Zuma.

"Silas, I want you to meet Zuma Gambris, our weapons expert." Zuma took his hand quickly to shake it, and then backed away looking nervous.

"I see you are having fun with the weapons." Zuma said with a slight Scottish accent.

"Yeah, this is a great collection."

Vik spoke up then. "I want you to train with Zuma." He said a bit awkwardly as though he was afraid of what Silas's reaction would be. Silas considered this and could think of no objection. He really wanted a chance to test out the unknown weaponry, and learn more about their capabilities.

"When do I start?" He said, smiling as he swung the bat through the air again, causing Vik to take a few steps back grinning.

"Perfect! Perfect! You can start first thing tomorrow, if you like. Unless that's too soon..."

"No, it's perfect." Silas interrupted, and Vik beamed.

"Well, in that case, we had better be going. There's a lot more to see!" Vik turned and bowed to Zuma, who lowered his head into a slight returning bow.

"Nice to finally meet you." Zuma said to Silas as they shook hands again.

"Of course, be ready for me tomorrow." He saw a hint of fear cross Zuma's face, so he grinned, attempting to look friendly.

"See you then." Zuma said as they left toward the tunnel entrance.

"Next!" Vik consulted the map. "I think I'll show you the western gardens, Yes." Vik shoved the map back into his pocket, and then trudged forward. They came to an opening where the sun streamed in from the other room.

The tunnel split into a fork – Vik led him to the right without hesitation. He slowed as they walked into a small room. A couple of people stood beside three or four, one-man, air powered range cars. They had four large wheels and a small seat in the center. Silas noticed each of the steering wheels was equipped with its own touch screen computer.

"We'll need two." Vik said, and the men went to work moving two range cars out into the center of the room.

"Ah perfect." Vik said, examining the two cars. "We'll have them back before dark."

"No, this one is a gift for our guest." Said a

short man with a thick, rough voice. Silas opened his mouth to protest, but the man stopped him before he could continue. "Trust me sir, this will be of great use to you."

Silas could tell by the look on the man's face that arguing would be useless – so he just smiled and thanked him before climbing onto the leather seat of the range car. It looked new, and he could not imagine how they had brought it to the cave.

Vik boarded his car and pushed a few buttons on the touch screen computer. It beeped several times, and then his car began to move forward. Silas was just about to explain that he had never driven a range car, when it started moving forward completely on its own.

It followed Vik's car steadily out into the tunnel. Silas heard the men laughing behind him as he left. He was sure they had seen the panicked look on his face.

The two cars began moving faster once they entered the tunnel, fast enough to make Silas grin despite himself. The wind pushed his hair back flat against his head, and caused his eyes to water. He was griping the seat tightly as they swung around the sharp corners. It was causing his body to sway dangerously over the edge of his seat. Vik seemed totally unaffected by the turns – he sat straight up, holding the steering wheel lightly in one hand and checking the map in the other.

They passed a few small rooms where Silas could see people moving inside. He caught glimpses of them before zooming past. Silas assumed they must be traveling through more living quarters.

He was starting to worry that they would run into someone in the tunnel, but they never did. Finally, they slowed down. It happened so quickly that Silas almost flew forward off his seat.

Vik steered his car sharply into the opening of the garden room like a professional. This had to be the biggest room yet, and by far the most striking. The entire ceiling was open to the sky, protected of course, by the unbreakable glass which kept the two worlds separated.

The rest of the room was covered in plants, and flowers unlike any he had ever seen. Machines swooped over the flowers every few seconds and sprayed them with a misty haze.

Silas was still gripping his seat when he noticed Vik beside him laughing. Stepping up to Silas's car, Vik pushed a small green button on the side. Instantly, thin metal clamps rose up and around his calves, clamping him tightly to the sides of the car. Silas looked at them, feeling a little stupid. Then Vik pushed the red button beside the green one and the metal clamps flew off.

Silas climbed off his car, not taking his eyes away from the amazing scene before him. Vik had already moved into the gardens – Silas walked quickly to catch up. They walked into one of the wide rows, the green mist coating his face.

"Magnificent isn't it?" Vik said, bringing Silas back to reality.

"How does it work? Where does the water come from?" Silas said fervently. He was still staring around at the amazing, brightly-colored plants. Some even moved around in their pots, holding their leaves toward the sky, absorbing whatever sunlight they could reach.

"We aren't sure. It was this way when we arrived."

"But how? It can't run on its own. Can it?"

Vik laughed again. "Well, I guess it can. It has been taking care of itself since we found it. The plants are fed and watered by this room. When one dies, the machines take it away." Vik pointed to a small metal hatch in the ceiling.

"We have tried to get up there to open it. But

it too, is impenetrable." Vik shook his head. "This room is by far, the most miraculous thing we have discovered about the cave."

"I can see why." Silas said, moving toward a large plant that looked like a human face. He was about two feet from it when the eyes blinked slowly, then separated into a million tiny flowers that danced around in their immense flower pot.

They moved around in circles until they began forming another face. Silas watched for a while until he noticed that the face was his. One small flower in the center of each eye was spinning around, mimicking his swirling pupils.

"Amazing." He whispered.

The little plants rearranged again to form the word he had just said with its flower-petal lips.

"Those are shifters. We found that most of the plants are labeled. That one is always a point of interest on tours." Vik said, leaning against a tall plant whose long, smooth blades made it look exactly like giant blades of dark green grass.

Vik stroked the plant once and it purred softly at him. Once he stopped, it nudged his arm until he continued.

"We don't know the name of this one. But it's

extremely friendly." He laughed as the plant sagged in its pot, enjoying the massage. Silas moved forward when he noticed a gigantic purple plant. It was dancing around gracefully, swaying back and forth and then twirling.

"I wouldn't, if I were you." Vik said. Silas stopped at once.

"What is it?" He said while watching the plant continue to dance.

"We don't know the name of it. But when we came here one of the small boys nearly lost an arm." Vik plucked a bunch of grapes from his pocket and tossed it at the dancing plant. The plant was doing an elaborate set of back flips when the grapes soared above it.

At once, so quickly that he almost did not see it. The plant spun in midair – a set of enormous fangs appearing from the depths of its ornate petals.

It ate the entire batch of grapes in one bite before continuing to dance as if nothing had happened. Silas just watched in shock as the plant danced innocently before him.

"So much for my snack..." Vik said. He pulled a spare grape from his pocket and popped it in his mouth. "Well, we need to be going." But Silas did not want to leave the gardens, he had seen so little.

Vik however, was already climbing onto his range car. Silas hurried over, climbing onto his car and pressing the green button.

He watched the little metal arms fly up and over his legs, holding them firmly against the car. Then they were moving again, flying through the dark tunnel so fast his eyes struggled to adjust.

It was only a few seconds later that they slowed. They turned another tight corner into a stone room. This room was much different than the garden. It seemed warmer, with its dark wooden furniture, and a crackling fire set inside a prodigious stone fireplace. But most of the space was taken up by ancient wooden bookshelves.

These shelves were stacked with piles of books that looked just as old, if not older, than the shelves that held them.

It was a comfortable room, the warm feeling of relaxation filling it completely. Silas wanted to go straight for the overstuffed armchair by the hissing fire and never leave.

"This is our library. These books are

extraordinary." Vik said as he pulled an old leather-bound book from the shelf nearest him. He unfolded its torn pages showing it to Silas. On the page was an old picture of an enormous beast. He had never seen anything like it, the creature was gray and rough-looking; it appeared to have no hair apart from tiny stubs on its tail. Also the proportions seemed all wrong, the ears were enormous, and the nose unnaturally long.

It had tusks like the pig beast he fought in the tunnel, but the eyes were different, gentle, and almost wise in the way it stared from the page. Underneath the picture was the caption *African Elephant.* Vik folded the book shut and handed it to him.

"We don't know how these got here either." He said strolling along the aisles, grabbing the occasional book to look through. "Thousands of years of history; history that we haven't even been taught since the government started limiting what we could learn about."

Silas looked at the front cover of the old book in his hands. Another exotic-looking creature was depicted on the front, stamped into the leather.

It was human-like, but it stood on all fours supporting itself with two colossal forearms. It was covered in thick, black fur which turned into a lighter color on its back. He wanted to look through the book to see what the animal was called, but Vik interrupted him.

"This is one of the more unique entries we have found in the library."

Vik handed him another leather-bound book. As he opened it, a few pages fell out – Silas caught them before they touched the ground.

The book was not just a book, it appeared to be some kind of journal. The pages were full of messy handwriting, scrawled on the front and back of every page. There were hundreds of pages smashed together in complete disarray.

"What is this?" He turned the brimming book over in his hands a couple of times. He wondered where the safest place to start would be.

"It's a journal, but not an average journal. It contains some fascinating recordings of what might just be on the outside." He glanced through the window; the sun was beginning to set.

"If it has so much valuable information, why aren't you keeping it someplace safe?" Silas asked mostly to himself.

"Not many people come here. Half of the

younger people can't even read. I thought you would find them useful, if you can make out what it says." Vik retrieved two more books from the shelves, and Silas took them happily.

"As far as we can see, a few pages of the journal seem to be missing. But that is natural, considering the state it's in."

"So, is this it?" Silas said looking around the library.

"Goodness no, but the rest of the cave is mostly private quarters. There are a few small private gardens as well."

"This place is amazing." Silas said as they walked back to the cars.

"Oh yes, now if we could only find the book in here that explains the reason it exists." Vik said with a sigh.

"The reason for somethings existence is not always found in a book, you know." Silas put the books on the back of his range car and fastened the straps.

"All too true, my friend."

***

By the time they had wheeled into the cave where the cars were stored, it was nearly dark in the tunnel. The range car's lights clicked on dimly as Vik played with the controls. The short man from before was waiting on them, the other two had gone.

Vik handed the man something, though Silas could not see what. He assumed some kind of payment for the cars. Then Vik waved to the man and set off down the dark tunnel. Silas was carrying a stack of books in his arms.

As they walked, he could not help but glance down at the cover of the book on top, the big, hairy creature staring back at him with almost human eyes. Not just human, but also revealing some emotion that appeared majestic and proud. They walked back to Vik's quarters, stopping in front of the entrance.

"I hope this satisfies some of your curiosity. There is a lot more of course, as I said. But you have seen all of the most important parts."

"There is still one question I need answered." Silas said – Vik raised his eyebrows. "I know how to get in. But I still don't understand how to get out."

Vik dropped his eyes to the floor; he seemed to

be thinking something over. Finally, he raised his head. Silas saw something in his eyes that sent a shiver down his spine. It was the first time since he had arrived that he had seen something untrustworthy in Vik. They both looked at each other.

"You can't leave."

Silas didn't know what to say. He felt something oddly similar to rage building up inside him.

"What do you mean, I can't leave? You know the way out, you have to."

Vik was quiet for a moment before he replied. "We can't risk them finding you and taking you back."

The sound of Silas' laughter seemed to shake the cave walls around them.

"Take me! You must know better than that!"

"You don't understand. We need you, especially if it comes down to a fight."

"I understand." Vik only stared at him then. "But you can't keep me here. If I want to leave, I will. It would be better for you not to fight me."

Vik sighed and ran a hand across the back of his thick neck. "I don't want to fight you, but you cannot leave unless you know how. To try and leave when you do not understand how the cave works could be disastrous."

"Then show me how!"

"Why would you want to leave!?" Vik shouted. "We have everything we need here!"

Silas slammed his hand into the cave wall sending a crack to the ceiling. Vik watched the crack with amazed eyes as it traveled overhead.

"Listen, I don't want to leave permanently, I just think that..." He was going to say he should try finding his friends, but he decided different. "I think that we need more information on what is going on out there, something more reliable than what they are giving us on the news." Vik didn't say anything. Instead he continued watching the crack on the ceiling.

"And we both know I am the perfect person to do it. I'm stronger and faster than anyone here."

Vik sighed again and looked at him. "One condition." He said in a tired voice. Silas felt a ping of annoyance toward Vik for trying to make bargains with him.

"What?" Silas said through gritted teeth.

"You have to use your talents to help us break

out." He glanced up at the crack in the ceiling again. Small bits of rock were crumbling from the fracture.

Silas felt like disagreeing. Something about the way the entire cave seemed like a fortress from whatever lurked outside made him want to keep it secured. It seemed like that door needed to stay closed, and he did not want to be the one held responsible for opening it.

But this feeling could not surpass the urgency he felt toward finding his friends. They had, after all, done everything they could for him. They spent everything they had to find him the necessary tools needed to break into the lab and steal the weapon before the worst could happen.

He could not leave them behind – not like the government had done to him, and to all of them that still waited hopelessly for a rescuer. Silas looked at Vik who was waiting patiently by the entrance to his quarters.

"Fine," Silas said. Vik relaxed noticeably.

"Now, bedtime I think." He smiled, then turned and strolled down the hallway without looking back at Silas. "Don't forget your lessons tomorrow." Silas heard Vik say through the darkness.

Silas took his time returning to his own room. His mind was busy thinking of any way he could get out of the bargain. He could feel it, something deep inside telling him it was all a very bad idea.

But then again *how trustworthy is a feeling like that?* He was not sure if he could trust himself any more than he could trust Vik. Silas looked down at his dust-colored hands in the darkness as he walked. The new muscles flexing when he wiggled his fingers. *Who had he become? And was that person trustworthy?*

When he made it back to his room, Silas immediately noticed movement under the timeworn bed. The shock caused him to freeze on the spot.

He stood completely silent without moving or breathing. Whatever was under the bed had noticed him, because it froze too. Silas could hear the steady thrum of a heartbeat; he knew at once that this was no animal.

In a flash he tore across the room. He thrust one hand under the bed, grabbing a fist full of something soft. He tugged hard before his arm returned to the surface – the silence around him was broken by a high-pitched scream of terror.

TWENTY-THREE

When he raised his arm, Silas was shocked to find a girl dangling from it – her legs kicking in midair and her arms flailing around. He felt his eyes bulge as he took in her face. He knew her.

She was still kicking when he let go of her shirt, which sent her flying backwards on the floor. Breathing hard she looked up at him, her eyes reflecting the confusion in his. He was sure she did not recognize his new face, her eyes were wide and guarded.

She was backing away from him toward the entrance, standing up to run. But he was in front of the entrance before she had taken two steps. She slammed into him, and then bounced off, landing back on the floor.

She looked at him for several minutes through a thick main of tangled, black hair. Her breath was ragged, then she went quiet. She was not breathing, only staring at him, the shock flitting across her face.

"Si?" She whispered, her voice sounded harsh

and dry as if she had not had anything to drink for some time.

"It's me Terra." Silas spoke.

Her face went white, and then she stood slowly. Her approach was slow, but she finally made her way to him. They looked warily at each other, each wondering what the other would do next.

"I'm not going to hurt you, you know that." He was looking at her seriously, hoping that she could see through his appearance.

Then she flew at him. He thought at first she was going to run for the exit. But she ran straight into him, hugging him tighter than anyone ever had.

"I thought you were dead." She sobbed into his shirt. "I thought they took you away from us. I thought they made you into a monster." She raised her head, tears leaving streaks of grime on her face. "But here you are. I can see it's you." She smiled and then buried her face into his chest again.

He hugged her until she stopped crying and pulled away. Gathering herself and marching across the room, she plopped onto his bed.

"You have a lot of explaining to do." She said, a little smile crossing her face. She patted the space beside her and Silas obeyed, sitting down next to her.

"I'm sorry." he said. She looked at him, her face was almost sad. "That is all I can say."

"I know. I'm sorry too." She looked down at her dirty fingers.

"What could you have to be sorry about?" Silas laughed. Her eyebrows came together and she swallowed.

"I should have gone with you." She looked him over again, taking in his appearance.

"I chose this." he said, gesturing at himself. "I couldn't save you the way I was before."

She shook her head, but it seemed like she didn't want to argue.

"It's over now, you're alive." She smiled at him, one of those real smiles that he loved so much. He felt his strong heart skip as she reached out her dirt-covered hand and put it on his.

Their hands looked odd together. His the color of a desert at night, hers hidden beneath layers of dirt and filth – so small and fragile-looking. He felt his heart sink when he pulled his hand away. He could not stand to look at their hands together; they had become so different from one another. Terra pretended not to notice the moment of tension, instead she hopped off the bed to rummage underneath it.

She returned moments later hauling an old leather bag. It was so full that it looked like it might explode at any moment. She tossed it easily onto the bed where it bounced chaotically before settling down.

"What is it?" Silas said looking at the bag.

"My travel pack." She said brightly, unzipping the front pocket. Several items fell out, including a piece of paper which she handed to him. "Now that I've figured out how to get in, I need to find out how to get out." She jumped back onto the bed, causing several more items to fall onto the floor from the over-stuffed bag.

He looked at the paper in his hands. It was a hand-drawn map, and he could not recognize any of the landmarks depicted.

"I don't understand." He said, turning it over in his hands as if some other piece of the map would appear magically. "Is this it?"

Terra looked pleased with herself as she

scooped the map from his hands. "By out, I don't mean back to where we came from." She smiled an evil grin, and something clicked inside his head.

"You want to get out there!" He pointed a finger at the window where the stars had appeared in the sky.

"Yup." She looked excitedly back at him.

"That's impossible! Who gave you that map?" He tried to snatch it back from her, but she dodged him, stuffing the map down the front of her shirt.

"Very mature." He said as she laughed at him. He stood and turned his back to her breathing deeply.

"OK, OK, jeez don't get all worked up." He felt her walk up behind him. "We fled to the woods." Her tone was serious now. "It was the only way we could stay alive. The rescuers haven't destroyed the eastern forest yet."

"Why didn't you stay? They wouldn't have harmed you if you had just stayed with the rest of the camp."

"They caught a few of us snooping through the storage containers outside the landing area." Silas turned toward her. Her face was serious, theft was forbidden. Anyone who committed it would be killed, or sentenced to prison. She noticed his expression and then quickly added.

"By caught, I mean they *saw* us. They didn't actually catch us."

"Who? How many of you were seen?"

"Just me... and Finx...and Quartz." Silas was not surprised by this. Finx and Quartz were twins – and equally demented. They could escape just about any situation if they wanted, and they were both incredibly clever.

"Then where are they? I haven't seen any of you since I've been here."

"They are still on the surface. I told them to wait for me." She held the map in her hands, attempting to flatten the wrinkled corners with no success.

"But who gave you that map?" Silas said, pointing at it.

"Well..." She looked around the room thinking of exactly what to say.

"We sort of made some friends – they got us away from the RT." Silas raised his eyebrow as she continued. "After our first few nights of running in the woods, we were getting tired, and nervous. The

RT had us surrounded in the forest; it was just a matter of time until they found us." She paused, rolling the map up and then unrolling it over and over.

"Then we saw this kid. He was running through the trees. He was only a little younger than us, we followed him."

Silas felt his muscles tense. He had seen a boy in the forest; it was the same one, he knew it must be. Terra sat down on the floor crossing her legs and leaning forward toward him. He sat down in front of her as she continued.

"Anyway, he helped us hide in the cave – told us everything."

"What do you mean *everything*?"

"He told us how the cave worked, and about the other world." She said this so casually it almost made him laugh.

"Other world, eh?" He chuckled.

"It's true." Her eyes told him no lie. She was certain and he could see that. "They have been trying so hard, incredibly hard, just to stay alive – spending everything to end up on that man-made piece of junk." She pounded the floor with her fist in frustration. "But it's here! Somewhere around us is the world we need so badly. The earth is rebuilding itself."

Silas did not understand exactly what she meant by this. He thought about it for a while before he spoke.

"You think the world isn't over yet?"

She laughed, "No, I think the world we knew before is over. What I think is that the door has been opened, and we have been given something great."

"But, what if it's not true? You can't tell me that you believe this just because some jungle boy said so." She looked at him amazed.

"You can't sit here and tell me, you don't believe something weird is happening. Look for yourself!" She pointed at the window; stars were glinting over a cloudless sky. Something he had never seen until his stay here.

"But it's dangerous! It has to be! Someone built this place to keep something out."

"Maybe it is, but that is not why this place was built." She leaned forward again keeping her eyes focused on him. "It's meant to keep us in." She stood then, and Silas was by her side in a flash.

"You think that someone is trying to keep people from knowing about what's out there?" He asked.

"Absolutely. Not only do I think, I know."

"You do? Well why didn't you say so earlier?"

She snickered. "I heard Vik talking to a member of his team this morning."

"How do you know Vik? I thought you just got here?" She laughed again, grabbing his shoulder for support.

"Of course I do, I followed you in when you first came here." She said this like it was nothing of importance – if not utterly obvious.

"Anyway, Vik said something about how it was important to keep the cover – not let *him* figure out the real exit. Of course I knew exactly who they meant when they said *him*." Silas pointed at himself, and Terra smiled.

"So what is your plan then? If we are going to break out of here, we don't want to cause a fight." Silas thought about how much he would love to test his new body in battle. But he pushed the thought out of his mind.

"I think we should do it now." She said casually.

"Now!? What do you mean *now*!?"

He couldn't believe she would want to try and break out of the protection of the cave in the middle of the night, when they had no idea what was waiting for them on the other side.

"Well, why not? We have everything we need. If we can get out before they notice you're gone – well, they wouldn't be able to find us out there."

"You don't know what's out there!"

"Yes I do." She was staring at him seriously again. "I told you, I've learned all about this place."

Silas could not argue with her, but he wanted to change her mind. He felt like breaking out now was a bad idea, especially with the tension building between him and Vik. He knew Vik would be suspicious of him. Surely Vik would have someone following him.

"What all did you learn, exactly?" He raised one eyebrow at her, she half-smiled.

"That can wait." And then she darted away. He watched her curiously as she ran around the room. Gathering things from the floor and tossing them into her bag.

When the bag had returned to its original,

plump state, she threw it over her shoulder and turned to him.

"So, we better get started. I know they have been guarding the supposed dig site, against anyone who might want to wander around..."

He stood and grabbed the small knife he had stashed away under his pillow.

"The question is how do we get past the Narkil without making a scene..."

Silas felt his muscles tense at the mention of the horrible creature in the Southern tunnels.

"Yeah, definitely don't want to make a scene."

"Lucky for us, Narkils have poor eyesight. We might be able to sneak by him, if we are careful."

Silas had no doubt that he could be completely silent if he wanted.

"Let's do it." He said, and she nodded.

They walked side-by-side down the dark dimly-lit passageway. It was completely deserted, as Silas had expected for dead of night. People were not allowed to wander around the caves at night, and they didn't want to, not with the Narkil around.

They made it to the dining hall which was also

deserted. Terra leaned forward peering around in the dark.

"I think it's clear, can you...?" She paused looking at him curiously. He could see her perfectly in the dark. Her face still covered in dirt.

"Can I what?" He smiled.

"I mean, the virus, it changed you, sort of enhanced your abilities, right?" Silas nodded slowly. "Can you see in the dark?" She asked.

"I can also hear everything." He said nodding.

She peeked out into the darkness again, squinting as if just being near him would give her night vision too. Then she looked back at him.

"Can you hear anything now? I just need to be sure."

He closed his eyes and absorbed the area around him, the sound of their hearts beating, and the slow combined thrum of their lungs working. It was so loud his head twisted with pain. Somewhere far-off he could hear someone snoring.

"It's clear." He whispered. She turned and walked slowly into the dining hall. Silas followed her closely. He was listening and watching for any sign of life, any sign that they were being followed. But there was no sign of life outside their own as they continued toward the Southern tunnels.

They were moving quietly and quickly along the wall. Silas noticed the sound of Terra's feet on the rocks; his steps made no noise whatsoever. He reached out and grabbed her shoulder, pulling her to a stop.

"It's going to hear us." She looked at him, her face confused.

"What do you mean?" She whispered.

"The Narkil will hear you. If I can, I'm sure he can." They both looked down at her feet.

"What should we do?" Terra asked. It happened so quickly, that there was only a flash of color and the sharp intake of Terra's breath as Silas threw her onto his back. She felt so light, she had never weighed much, but his new body was stronger than before. He hardly noticed her at all.

She clamped her arms around his neck as he moved silently down the tunnel. They both held their breath when the passage ahead began to curve. Silas knew that just behind the wall somewhere near the dig site was the Narkil.

It was chained, so it could not go too far from the site. Silas peered around the wall. The dig site was dimly lit with torches. The workers he had seen earlier were gone, probably in their quarters sleeping.

Silas felt relieved, and then he heard it, the sound of breathing, slow and steady. He could not tell exactly where it was coming from; the sound seemed to be bouncing off the cave walls in all directions. Neither of them took a breath as he stepped up to the cracked rocks.

He sat Terra gently on her feet, he was careful not to make too much noise. Terra stood completely still. She gestured toward one of the old pick axes leaning against the cave wall.

Silas crossed the room and picked up the axe, praying that the rock wall between him and the outside was a thin one. He heaved the axe behind his head, and then sent it plowing into the rock with a crack so loud that Silas felt the vibrations all the way to his skeleton. He had done it, rock was falling everywhere.

A rainstorm of pebbles and dirt poured down on them both. Silas could see a tiny hole revealing the night sky half-way up the cave wall. Just as he raised the axe again for a second strike, he heard a growl behind him.

"Si, watch out!" Terra screamed.

Silas instinctively swung around so fast that he was nothing but a blur. He felt his axe hit before he even saw what was happening. The creature howled. Silas saw his axe buried deep in the shoulder of the Narkil – blood pooled under its crouching body.

The creature reached out a clawed, furry hand and plucked the axe from its arm. Silas ducked as the Narkil swung a blow intended for his head. As he rose back up, the Narkil slammed a massive hand against his shoulder which sent him flying into the cave wall. The wall cracked, scattering rubble down to the floor. Silas got up as quickly as he could, but his shoulder screamed.

The pain from the impact caused his eyes to blur. The Narkil swung again and Silas dodged, missing the swing by inches. Suddenly, the Narkil howled, falling to its knees and growling loudly.

Silas spotted the handle of an axe protruding from the creature's furry back. Then he saw Terra standing behind the Narkil breathing heavily, her face half-hidden under her hair. She ran to him, picking up Silas's fallen axe.

"Hurry before he recovers." She gave him the axe. Silas climbed up the pile of rubble to the weak opening in the cave wall. Just as he slammed the axe against the stone he heard voices coming down the cave. Rock exploded everywhere, flying across the room and slamming into the cave walls.

Without thinking Silas took Terra's arm and threw her through the opening he had created in the cave. He could only hope that whatever was out there would be safer than what they would be leaving behind.

Silas was just crawling through the rubble when Vik appeared at the end of the room. Vik looked shocked, his face whiter than ever. He looked from Silas to the wounded Narkil on the floor, trying to understand the scene before him. Silas turned and rushed out of the cave leaving Vik to stand confused in the wreckage that had been his dig site.

Terra knelt at the edge of the grassy field waiting for Silas. When he approached she half-jumped, half-flew onto his back as he started running full speed toward a the group of thick trees ahead of them.

"They aren't following us!" Terra yelled into his ear. Silas glanced back; the people from the cave were standing at the edge, not moving. Terra was right. The group only stared dumbly as the two of them escaped into the forest. And then

Silas heard it, the sound of range cars blasting through the cave. Silas pushed forward, running to the safety of the trees ahead of them. He was nearly there when the range cars flew out into the open.

Silas felt Terra grip his shoulders even tighter as he ran faster, impressing even himself with the speed. Every muscle in his body was pushing him forward, but the range cars were gaining. Though he was very fast, Silas knew he could not outrun the range cars, no matter how hard he tried.

He hit the trees at full speed, twisting his body to dodge the dense branches. Suddenly the range cars slowed, they were having trouble getting through the crowded trees.

But Silas did not stop, instead he continued running until he found a tree big enough to hold them both. He sat Terra on her feet near a particularly large tree, its crooked branches reaching out to its forest brethren. Each branch was covered in leaves – the perfect camouflage.

"Hurry!" Silas urged Terra. She obeyed at once, hoisting herself quickly up the tree.

He did the same, settling beside her on a large twisted branch. He could hear the range cars die somewhere in the forest, then the sound of footsteps rustling leaves echoed around the tree trunks. Terra looked at him, her eyes reflecting the worry he felt.

They had always been that way, when he felt an emotion it was expressed on her face without saying a word. It was as though she simply felt the same emotions he did, at the same time.

The footsteps got closer, and Silas found himself hoping the refugees followed them without night vision. With such a device, they could easily be spotted from the tall tree. Silas held his breath as something moved through the trees. Something large and covered in black fur was heading toward them.

When the animal finally stepped out of the trees, it was near enough for him to see. Silas was amazed at the creature in front of him; it looked almost like a massive dog with beady, black eyes, and huge claws that stood out pale white against the dark foliage it stood on.

Its body seemed much thicker than a dog, or anything else Silas had ever seen. It paused near the tree and stood suddenly on its hind legs, raising its enormous head to sniff the air. Silas tried very hard to remain still, but everything inside him said to run. Glancing at Terra, he could see she felt the same. Her eyes were wide and her breath shallow.

The creature came closer to the tree. Slowly it raised itself up on the side, scraping its claws against the bark. A deep growl rumbled in the animal's furry chest as it sniffed the air again. Then suddenly, something else moved in the trees, and two men appeared. They looked like the workers who had been digging in the tunnel.

The men strolled forward holding silencers in their hands, but they stopped at the sight of the beast, taking several steps back.

It had turned to stare at them. Silas could see no fear – no emotion at all on the animals face. It simply watched them as if it were bored.

Then, without warning, it charged them, landing on top of the shorter man who fell back on the ground howling.

The taller man was just raising his gun to shoot when the beast swung a massive paw, knocking him to the ground. He fired two shots before the creature was on top of him. Silas could hear the man's muffled screams beneath the furry body.

Then suddenly the animal stopped attacking. It turned and wobbled a bit before falling over beside the man on the ground. The silencer was taking affect. The man on the ground stood and ran back out of the forest, leaving his friend behind.

Silas heard the sound of the range cars fading in the distance; he doubted the man would return. The short companion lay motionless on the ground, his face covered in blood. The beast was lying beside him, breathing heavily.

Silas dove from the tree, not bothering to climb down the limbs. He landed with a soft thump, and then waited for Terra to climb down. When she was beside him, they started running again, this time slow enough for her to keep pace.

"Over here!" Terra said, stopping suddenly after they had been running for several minutes. She moved to a thicket of bushes hidden deep beneath the tall trees. It would have to do, Silas thought, as he moved toward it.

"I think it might rain soon." She said, looking up through the trees at the dark sky where the stars had disappeared.

Silas allowed himself to breathe deeply for the first time since they had made their escape. He could smell it, faint and powerful all at once – it was the smell of a coming rain. This smell aroused something in his memory, but he could not place it. He had seen very few rain storms in his life.

Silas left Terra hidden in the trees as he went to find supplies for a shelter. He ripped several thick tree limbs from the furry green trees and hauled them back to their camp. Terra had already cleared a small area for them to lie inside – a bed for the night.

Silas worked for several minutes stacking the branches one against the other. Just as he laid the last one in place, something cold and wet landed on his skin. He ran his fingers over the spot. Looking closely, he saw a tiny drop of water reflecting the color of his skin. There was something enchanted about this tiny drop.

He saw them then high above the tree tops, well before they hit his skin. The rain began to pour down in gentle waves, soaking his clothes, and smacking against the leaves that extended from the branches overhead.

By the time he crawled inside the den of leaves, Terra was already curled up in the corner shivering from the cold brought on by the rain. Silas took the coat that she had spread out for his bed and handed it to her.

She hesitated at first, and then took it,

wrapping the fabric around her slender frame twice. She was so small and thin, Silas was afraid she would not survive the cold wet forest for long. But he knew more than anyone that Terra was stronger than she looked. She had always been that way.

Terra looked up at him and shivered again. "What do we do now?"

"I wish I knew." He said sadly.

"Well, let's think about this... The lab wants you back. Vik wants you back. The new government wants to kill you." She sighed, scooting closer to him.

"I am sort of popular these days." Silas said smiling.

"I think we should wait here. If everything goes as planned, the rest of the camp should be here soon."

"The camp?" Silas asked. Terra's face was pale in the darkness.

"Yes, the twins, and a few others were hiding in the woods. A couple of them already knew about this place. They have been trying to get in for weeks."

"How many are there?"

"About fifty. But most of them are not even on this planet."

Silas was stunned by this, none of it made sense. The refugees could not afford to live on NB1. "What do you mean? How?" he said quickly.

"They stole one of the Hilo lifts. It was months ago, the new government covered it up."

"But how could they stay undercover? Isn't New Blue sort of tight on security?"

"Well of course it is, but they don't expect that many people to sneak in illegally."

"You said yourself that the government knew about the group stealing the Hilo. They will be expecting something."

She sighed running a hand through her thick bushy hair. "Well, if you time it right, sneaking onto New Blue is not that hard."

Silas raised his eyebrows but he said no more on the subject. Instead he leaned back against the cushion of the thick bushes and closed his eyes. Terra moved closer, laying her head on his shoulder.

Silas wanted to run away from her, but he brushed the feeling aside. It was childish of him to be so effected by her touch.

But he wanted her away from him. He had been trying to avoid his feelings for so long, being around her made everything much harder. The time they had spent apart seemed to make him forget, but as soon as she showed up in the cave, everything was back to the way it had always been.

Slowly, he forced himself to ignore the warmness of her sleeping against his arm, her breath caressing his hand, and let his eyes flutter closed. It seemed like only a few minutes had passed when he woke, the light shining brilliantly through cracks in the branches overhead.

He was alone in the den of greenery. The night had been a short and dreamless one for once; his head did not throb for the first time in weeks. Silas crawled out of the bushes and stood.

Quickly surveying the area, he wondered where Terra had escaped to. Silas was not overly worried; he knew that if anything had happened his sensitive ears would have heard it.

But Terra was nowhere that he could see or hear, and the silent distance made him feel anxious. Then, just as he started to think something bad had happened, Silas heard the sound of chatter in the forest. There were several voices speaking seriously in low tones. They were getting closer and Silas took the moment to hide himself behind a tree.

He was hoping that Vik had not sent another group of scouts out to find them. Then he recognized Terra's voice among the babble and stepped out from his hiding place. Silas waited for them to appear in the clearing.

A short red-headed teenager stepped through the abundant trees first. He was thin, and his hair seemed to stick out at all angles. Behind him came another red-head – this time a girl. She was the same height as the boy, and clearly his twin.

Though they looked very similar, the girl's hair was long and straight, almost to her elbows. She looked him over suspiciously before turning to wait for Terra. When she appeared through the thicket, Terra smiled at Silas as he stepped closer.

Another teenage boy followed closely behind Terra, the stranger had jaw-length, midnight-colored hair, and pale, white skin. He was very tall, about the same height as Silas.

He looked at Silas curiously as he walked into the circle. Silas recognized him as the boy from the forest, the one he had followed the day he stumbled into the cave. The boy seemed very interested in Silas, but did not seem to recognize him.

Silas realized that the boy must not have seen the news. Everyone who had was far less affected by Silas's strange appearance. Finx and Quartz flashed identical evil grins when they finally realized who he was. Silas smiled back. He had know they would love his new appearance.

"Si, this is Sam." Terra said, gesturing toward the tall boy who walked over to shake his hand tightly.

Silas could see that he was trying very hard not to show the fear he felt. Silas gave him a smile, attempting to look friendly. Sam returned the smile half-heartily.

"Haven't I seen you before?" Silas said. Sam glanced at Finx, who nodded slightly.

"Um yeah, I sort of led you to the cave."

"Oh did you?" Silas said slowly.

"Well, Terra told me that if I saw you, I was to bring you to the cave. So I did." He was looking at the ground, absentmindedly pushing a rock around with his foot.

"So now we have to move on to the next stage." Terra spoke then.

"And that would be?" Silas said casually.

"Well, Sam is going to find us a proper camp. Quartz, you can go with him, you are good at that sort of thing."

"Then why can't I do it on my own?" Quartz said, his prominent red eyebrows pulling together.

"Because we need to go in teams, not all of us are as strong as Si." She smiled at Silas a little before continuing. "Finx and I will work out how to purloin one of the range cars."

"That shouldn't be too hard." Finx said smiling menacingly.

"It might be harder than you think Finx. Vik put trackers on all of the cars in the cave, just in case something like this happened."

"That has never stopped me before." Finx said smiling.

"Well then, it's settled. Silas, you are going back for the refugees. We need at least a few of them, if we stand a chance in this battle."

"What about the weapons they have? We have nothing." Silas spoke in a serious tone.

"We have you." Terra said, giving Silas a quick over-all glance. "If we can persuade the others to join us, think of the things we can accomplish."

Silas felt sadness wash over him for those who had been kidnapped and turned against their will, turned into monsters just like him. But they could be extremely helpful in a fight. Just a few mutants like him could take on an army of average men.

"I'll do what I can." Silas said. Terra nodded and then turned to Sam.

"Take this." She handed him two small bottles, one containing purple sand, the other bright orange. "If you need us pour these two on the ground, the signal should be strong enough for us to see no matter where we are out there."

Then Terra turned to Quartz. "Take good care of him, and please be careful. We don't know everything that is out there." Quartz bowed without saying a word, then turned to stroll through the trees.

Sam started to follow Quartz, but then stopped, turning toward Silas, his face whiter than ever.

"Can I talk to you for a minute?" He whispered and Silas nodded, moving into the trees so the others could not hear. Silas looked at Sam's pastel face. His eyes were underlined with deep purple, and he looked exhausted.

"Can I ask you a favor?" As Sam spoke, his

voice revealed a hint of fear. Silas considered this for a moment. Sam had already done Silas a favor by bringing him to the cave. He deserved a favor of his own. Going against the government to help a wanted man was very brave.

"Absolutely." Silas said, and Sam relaxed noticeably.

"Well, I have a friend, she is on NB1. I need you to bring her back, when you come back here." Sam looked at his feet again. "Please." He whispered. "I need her here." As Sam looked back at him, Silas could not help but feel sad for the boy.

"OK, but how will I find her?" Silas asked.

"Her mother owns the only machine factory on New Blue. I sent her a note several weeks ago, but she hasn't shown up. That is why I'm asking you. I know Vadell, and she would be here if she could. Something is stopping her from coming..." He bowed his head, shaking it back and forth.

"So her name is Vadell. Do you think she would tell me her name, if I asked?"

"Probably not. And yeah, her name is Vadell Monroe. But trust me you will know her when you see her. She is not like anyone else." Silas sighed as he remembered what it felt like to fall in love, and then he shrugged it off. He definitely didn't want to think about that.

"OK." he said taking Sam's hand and griping it tightly. "I give you my word. I will find her and bring her here." Sam shook his hand and nodded. They walked back to the circle without talking, and then Sam trotted off in the direction Quartz had gone.

"Hey Terra, I'll be gathering the supplies. Meet you at the stream in half an hour?" Finx asked as she skipped into the trees.

"OK." Terra called over her shoulder as she approached Silas.

She was standing in front of him looking almost sad. It was the same look she had given him that night before he left on his journey to the lab. He swallowed hard trying to avoid any emotion. Terra said nothing but closed the gap between them in two strides, pulling him into a tight hug.

"Promise you will make it back." Her voice was full of emotion.

Silas was silent for a minute. He did not want to make that promise, the one he knew he wouldn't keep. Tightening his arms around her shoulders he whispered; "Promise." They stayed like that for several minutes, neither of them wanting to let go.

Then finally Terra pulled away. Her face was only a few inches from his, and he could see the streaks of dirt where the tears had been on her cheeks.

"Goodbye." She said as she looked at him, her voice trembling. Suddenly, she turned away, running through the trees and away from him.

Silas stood there watching as she disappeared, listening to the sound of her feet against the forest floor. It was the saddest sound he had ever heard, his heart tugged against his chest, threatening to burst out.

Silas forced himself to focus – to push her from his mind was the only way he could survive. Instead, he focused on getting into the cave. He would have to go in the same way he had come out, that was the only option. He needed to get in without being seen, which he knew would be difficult, if not impossible.

But he knew exactly why Terra had picked him for the task. He was stronger than all of them, he could walk right by them and they could do nothing to stop him.

But he did not want to fight them, he knew that if that happened someone would die. So he drove the thought from his mind and began to run. He was heading back to the place that he hated, back to his home, and his prison.

He skidded to a halt when he neared the edge of the tree line. He did not see or hear any sign of life, but this meant very little, he knew they would be guarding the entry. Silas waited for another minute or two before he darted across the open, empty landscape.

He ran toward the mound of jagged rocks protruding from the ground. Silas took a deep breath, letting his senses do the work, absorbing anything and everything around him.

This was his favorite technique for detecting another person near him, and it was always accurate. As he focused he could hear it, the soft breath of a person inside the entrance of the cave. He knew there would be more soon.

There was only one way to get through – he had to run. And run he did, in a matter of seconds he had reached the cave, diving into the crumbly, broken fissure he had created.

As he soared through the crumbled rock Silas caught a glimpse of a man. He was sleeping in the corner as Silas rushed by, too silent to wake him. Silas hurried down the dark passageway; knowing that few people traveled the Southern tunnels made him feel more relaxed.

However, there would be very little he could do, once he reached the dining hall, since it was so frequently occupied. Unfortunately, he had no choice; the dining hall was his only connection to the other tunnels, and his only way out.

And so he ran quietly, but so fast he was only a blur of color against the stone passage. He approached the dining hall, inside was the sound of excited chatter, people discussing their daily events over a warm meal. It seemed that Silas had ended up in the dining hall just after lunch.

This worked to his advantage as he skimmed along the edge of the massive room. Most did not notice him, but the ones who did seemed uninterested in making a scene.

He knew it would not be long though, until one of them told Vik they had seen him. When this happened he would not have much time. Silas darted quickly into the tunnel leading out to the hospital wing. Once he was safely inside the dark, empty passageway, he broke out full speed. Only a few seconds later he saw the bright light of the sunny hospital wing spilling into the tunnel. The light was so bright he had to blink several times to adjust.

Silas stopped in front of the hospital before peeking around the corner to make sure it was clear. Inside, Ben was sitting on a wooden stool near a tall, thin desk. He was looking over some papers, his bulky round glasses perched on his porky nose. Ben seemed completely unaware of Silas as he continued to read his papers.

"I need your help." Silas said suddenly, causing Ben to jump and spin around in his seat.

His eyes bulged beneath his magnified spectacles when he caught sight of Silas. He looked as though he did not believe what he was seeing. He blinked several times trying to determine the state of his reality.

"But how..." Ben started and then faded off.

"Listen, Vik is trying to keep me here, but not for any good reason. I need you to help me get out." Silas explained quickly.

"But, if we are caught..." Ben said, his face going white.

"Don't worry, if they catch us, you can explain how you were trying to stop me." Ben seemed incapable of speech. He rocked his head back and forth, but not in protest. Ben stood finally, and pulled off his white coat.

"If we are going to do this, we need to do it now." He said as he strolled past Silas who followed him without question.

They headed down the tunnel back toward the dining hall. Silas was dreading the next part; Vik would notice if he made a second appearance. But he had hoped, that most of the crowd would have cleared out, including Vik. When they arrived at the dining hall it was mostly empty to his relief. But as they moved swiftly across the room to the only tunnel Silas had not seen, he recognized one of the remaining men huddled in the corner.

It was the very man who had escaped the creature in the woods. His friend had been killed, but he had retreated. The man noticed Silas. They looked at each other briefly before the man's face twisted in anger. He pushed away from his companion and pulled a silencer from his pocket.

Silas noticed that Ben was already ahead of him, jogging down the tunnel. As Silas followed, he was surprised by the speed at which Ben was able to run. Though he was quite old, he seemed to be in impressive shape.

When he reached Ben's side, Silas glanced over his shoulder just in time to see their pursuer raise his silencer to aim at the back of Ben's head. Silas focused quickly, allowing his mind to absorb the gun.

He listened for the clicking of the mechanisms inside when the dart flew from the weapon. He focused his power to his eyes and pushed it out toward the dart – it was something he had never tried before. He was scared suddenly, not knowing what would happen.

The dart had barely made it out of the gun when it exploded into a thousand tiny shards of silver. The gun flew from the man's hand, and landed with a loud thunk on the cave floor. Silas heard the man curse as he scrambled to pick up the fallen weapon.

They kept on running, faster than before. Ben led him to a small room unlike any other room he had seen in the cave. It had no natural light at all, but the entire room glowed red-orange from torches mounted on the walls in rows.

The torches went all the way up, to the very top of the high ceiling. Silas was stunned by this room, not because of its peculiar lighting, but because of what he saw before him.

In the center of the room was a giant swirling orb, appearing like the sky before a wicked tempest. It was black, gray, and red, all swirling together in one immense circle.

The orb rose into the air with immeasurable height, it was unlike anything Silas had seen before. He could not force it to make sense in his mind. The giant swirl seemed to have a thin glass surface that reflected his face, his eyes swirling in time with the colors in the orb.

"Now! He's almost here!" Ben shouted. Silas could hear the footsteps coming down the tunnel, but he could not leave Ben to deal with the armed mad-man alone.

Ben looked at Silas, his eyes pleading with him to hurry, but Silas stood frozen to the spot. The man whirled into the room, his gun raised toward Silas. Pure rage flowed through the desperate man's features. Silas felt a sudden burst of anger flood his veins, the full extent of his own power surging behind his eyes. Suddenly, a blast of green light filled the space – it seemed to be coming directly from Silas himself.

The green light became so powerful that Silas was almost blinded by it. He had never felt so intensely angry – *and for what purpose?* It happened so quickly that Silas could not understand. Ten long tentacles burst from his eyes – flying out of their own accord. The tentacles penetrated right through the man's body.

The man cried out before going limp, suspended in the air by jagged tentacles. The tentacles themselves were thin, and transparent as they slithered away from the man, who fell to the floor with a sickening thump.

Silas relaxed, the anger that fading was replaced by something else he did not recognize. The tentacles slinked back into his eyes leaving a transparent haze that lingered for only a second before his vision cleared.

Silas was breathing hard, sudden fatigue washed over him. He had been tired from shredding the gun, but it was nothing compared to what he felt once the tentacles had dissipated. Silas fell to his knees, his head throbbing. As they sat there in silence, Ben seemed to be too stunned for words.

Silas opened his eyes and looked at the man on the ground. The green tint still lingered around the body of the man, who was lying in a bloody pool on the hard cave floor. Silas's head throbbed again. He closed his eyes, holding his head with both hands. *He had killed someone.*

"You need to hurry. They will be coming soon." Ben said with a shaking voice. Silas obeyed, ignoring the pain in his head.

With knees wobbling, Silas walked toward the swirling mass in front of him. He used every ounce of energy he had left to walk across the room. First, he stumbled back; the reflection on the surface was terrifying.

It took him a second to realize that the reflection was his own. Silas could see his face, the dull skin, the strong features, but the reflection was different. His swirling pupils were glowing green, the veins around his eyes had popped to the surface; they too were shining visibly beneath his skin.

Silas thought he might collapse. Amazingly, his feet carried him until he hit the surface of the orb. He caught one last glimpse of his own chilling face before he fell, flying through a dark tunnel of swirling shadows.

TWENTY-FOUR

It was all very disorienting. He could not seem to get his mind straight on anything that was happening. His head throbbed as he swirled around in the darkness, which caused his stomach to churn. Silas was starting to feel weaker as he fought to hold on to his consciousness. He watched the green glow float around his head – it seemed to be fading.

Abruptly, he slammed into something solid. The impact shook his bones. Silas felt like his brain had popped loose and was floating around in his skull. The dark room was spinning worse than ever. It took him much longer than usual to adjust to the total darkness.

Finally, Silas realized he was in a cave, though his foggy brain had a difficult time understanding why he was there. He stumbled through the darkness, only knowing that he needed to keep moving.

Silas staggered on until his body could take no more. He slipped, falling between two large boulders. He lie there until everything started to fade away – welcoming the rest he so desperately needed. He wanted nothing more than to feel the serenity of sleep.

Slowly he drifted into nothing, and then nothing turned into something as his dreams began pouring out – a mixture of unintelligible colors and shapes.

All of a sudden, Silas could see the dead man in a pool of blood. The image swayed chaotically, dancing like the beautiful and deadly plant he had seen in the cave gardens.

Then the image flew away. Terra appeared then, hugging him tight and speaking in her sad voice. He could not understand her, though he tried hard to comprehend the mumble of sound.

After a few seconds, Terra disappeared, her face replaced by the doctor. His appearance seemed to have been distorted by time as he grinned evilly, opening his hands to reveal a tiny fireball.

The peculiar object exploded, showering Silas with fire and sparks. The dream went on for what felt like forever. Silas heard someone screaming in the distance, a sound that woke him from his sleep. He looked around for the cry he had heard in the dark cave – when suddenly, he realized the scream had been his own. It echoed off the walls, becoming more unfamiliar as it died away slowly.

Silas could see a small light gleaming somewhere ahead, he wanted badly to get up and run to it, to escape the dream that was already gone.

But his legs seemed to be asleep – they would not obey him when he tried to stand. He was tired, though he felt slightly better than before. His head still ached dully as he ran his cool hand across his face.

The cave was silent. Silas assumed that since he was still alive, nobody had discovered his hiding place while he slept. He could hear the familiar dripping of water in the cave, and was reminded of how dry his mouth was.

After several minutes of coaxing, he pulled himself to his feet and walked slowly toward the sound of the dripping water. After a minute or two he spotted a small indention in the cave floor, in it was a rippling pool of clear water.

Silas dove for it, scooping handfuls of water into his parched mouth. The sensation was amazing; his whole body seemed to wake up as the tiny droplets slithered down his throat, rejuvenating his tired muscles.

Silas drank until the puddle was nearly empty, and then continued down the cave, toward the glowing light ahead of him. He could smell the choking scent of smoke burning his nose and constricting his lungs as he walked.

When he reached the end of the cavern, Silas knew what he would see, though he did not want to believe it. Emerging from the cave, he wasn't sure if he was in the right place. Smoke filled the air, hiding many of the trees from view.

Somewhere inside Silas had known this would happen, but he had avoided the thought at all costs. He needed to hold on to hope. The hope that he still had a way to NB1.

Ignoring the smoke, Silas pushed his way through the trees, toward the edge of the forest where he hoped his abandoned craft would still be waiting for him.

Silas could not see the fire, but he knew it must be close. The smoke was getting thicker, and his lungs worked painfully as he ran. Silas was gliding through the forest, dodging tees, and leaping over fallen logs.

He suddenly burst from the tree line, much quicker than he had anticipated. Silas looked desperately for his craft, but he could not see it, the smoke was too thick. He took a guess at its location and darted off.

Miraculously, Silas spotted the silver gleam of a propeller blade, he smiled to himself as he ran to it. Pulling the door open, he flung himself inside.

From the driver's seat he could see almost nothing through the dense smoke, though the open plains gave him little to worry about in terms of colliding with someone, or something. He flicked the switches and pressed down on the pedal, causing the Hilo craft to roar with long subdued life.

The propellers began to whirl around above him, cutting through the air and the smoke as they pushed the craft to rise. Silas soared into the sky, flying high above the dead grass and swirling smoke.

He wasted no time heading for the launch pad, though he would have to find a way to launch without getting caught. Silas flew until the smoke cleared, wondering what the Rescue Team would do if they found the cave. *Would they even bother searching it? And if they did, what would they do if they found the portal?*

Of course, the cave was very dark, and very deep. Silas doubted the RT would waste their time on something as commonplace as a drippy cavern. But the worry still remained, and Silas tried rigorously to block it out.

He hoped feebly that the rest of his camp had been successful in their missions, and that he would be successful in his. Silas was still unsure about persuading the others to join him in battle – those who shared his abilities. But it was his only chance to change things for the better.

And yet, the variables had changed. The revelation of the portal meant the plan to sneak onto NB1, and live in secret beneath the surface was futile. The world they needed so desperately had been beneath earth's surface all along.

The earth had been creating for itself a new start, and a new chance for life to continue. But it was beyond the minds of the multitudes to believe. Even Silas would have doubted the new world's existence if he had not seen it with his own eyes.

Unfortunately, this meant starting from scratch. Anything left behind would be lost forever. Silas wondered if there were other portals throughout the world.

Certainly there must be others – hundreds of thousands of people, all over the world, would find it hard to meet at one spot in any reasonable amount of time. The single portal could not be the only way out.

Silas ruminated over the possibilities as he flew over sector six. He was headed for sector one, the capital of what used to be the United States. It was a sort of home base for the government – or what was left of it at least.

It was also, unfortunately, home to the launch pad. This location made the launch pad much harder to gain access to. It was heavily guarded, and Silas had no plan of action. That thought made him twitch at the idea of breaking in. He had heard of the capital's brutality – of the unstable group that called themselves *leaders*.

The cruel earth government did not shy away from killing anyone who disobeyed the rules. The government was represented very differently on the news of NB1 however. The leaders of NB1 wanted to appear as though they were in alliance with the government of sector one.

To insure their residents knew this, they would broadcast images of the RT, and the amazing feats of humanity they had illustrated on earth.

This was a perfect example of everything else created by the government – it was all a lie. When Silas reached the edge of sector two, he landed on a stretch of open field a few miles away from the border. From here, he could scope it out without being seen.

Silas stepped out of the craft and looked down over the hill to sector one. It was brightly lit, with hundreds of buildings in the center. It appeared worn from the sand-storms that frequently tormented the area.

The sector was a layered ring of activity. The center bustled with life, while the outer most rings seemed completely dead. The sand of the desert had washed upon it, leaving deserted cars half-buried beneath layers of dust.

Houses sat empty, windows broken, and walls disintegrating into the earth below. Silas felt a strange sadness for the capital. The dramatic difference between the light and dark was staggering.

There was beauty in the tragedy however. Silas admired the fading sunlight as it washed across the sand. How many more days would these people see before the end? They were trying so hard to keep it alive, to keep the lights on. Of course the center of the capital was unusual in itself, just by being alive, by holding on so long. Silas looked across to the opposite side of the city where he spotted the tall, black fence surrounding the launch pad. All of the Hilo crafts were gone, sent back to NB1.

When Silas reached for his bag, his stomach went cold. He had not even noticed its absence. His bag of supplies had been left in the cave the day he had discovered the portal.

Silas looked back at the Hilo craft. He was alone in the desert, without the supplies he needed to break the fence. And he desperately needed to get through that fence.

The Hilo craft alone would not be ready for space travel without the launch pad. He could not break the atmosphere without the detachable engines. Silas looked at the launch pad, taking in the strong black metal fence, and the massive control box that was protected by an electric shield.

It would be impossible to get into the box unless you were a guard. The guards hands were injected with a microscopic key. This key allowed their hands to pass through the electric field without harm.

But maybe he didn't need a key, Silas thought to himself. He remembered before how the blades had sliced through the trees with such ease.

Would the blades cut through the metal of the fence? Silas could only guess at the outcome, but it was his only option. If the blades were destroyed, he would still have the side propellers left. Though he would not be able to fly with them for long, at least he would be flying, not falling.

"This plan is beginning to appeal to me..." He said aloud to himself. He watched the unsuspecting guard walk the perimeter of the fence. Not wasting another minute, Silas broke into a run and leaped into the Hilo craft.

He knew the time to act was right then. Thinking too long would make him question his judgment, and he had no time for that. The Hilo rose into the air, roaring so loudly that Silas wondered if anyone in the city had heard him.

He hovered for a minute, looking for the guards patrol car. Finally, he spotted it making the rounds on the other side of the city. Silas set the craft going at full speed toward the launch pad – his heart pounding in time with the whirling propellers.

Silas had rarely felt the strange mixture of terror and excitement that he felt in that moment as he gripped the steering wheel. He was flying over the capital, and not a single person seemed to notice. He smiled to himself as he watched the buildings pass beneath him, a flash of colors and textures.

Finally, he was there. He could see the launch pad buried beneath a shell of powerful steel fencing. The entire launch pad was covered to protect against any form of intruder, even those from the sky.

Silas revved the engine of the Hilo, blasting toward the fence at full speed. Releasing the steering wheel, he instinctively raised his hands to protect his head.

The Hilo slammed into the unyielding steel fence. Everything felt like slow motion. The world was spinning slowly around him as the Hilo's blades sliced through the fence.

Pieces of metal flew everywhere as a horrible screeching sound filled the air. His eyes absorbed the details as each chunk of propeller was thrown into the distance along with the tangled fence. Silas fell through the fencing and managed to land the craft on the launch pad.

Quickly, he pushed the door open and ran toward the big green button on the side of the launch pad. He panicked an instant before his fingers touched it. He had forgotten the green button might be electrified. But to his amazement, he felt no pain.

The lights flashed on as the top of the broken fence fell back, making room for the launch. Two metal engines on either side of the craft were being lowered. They were then attached to the sides near the mini propellers.

They latched on quickly and blasted to life. Silas ran back to the craft and jumped in just as the doors began lock-down. Two plastic guards lowered over his head, and around his chest, fastening him in tight. The whole craft began to shake as the two powerful engines prepared for takeoff. Flames shot from the engines, and Silas felt like the entire craft was heating up.

Suddenly, at least ten patrol crafts flew into the area around the gate. Several officers jumped out carrying an array of weaponry. But they were too late. The gate had sealed itself for launch – there was nothing they could do, and the craft had already started to lift.

At first Silas felt like he was rising very slowly, and then everything was a blur. He flew into the sky so fast that he was thrown back into the seat. Silas's stomach gave an excited leap as he headed toward the edge of the world.

He was free, he was leaving the world for the first time ever and it was thrilling – breathtaking. Silas watched in amazement as he blasted through the atmosphere and shot into the darkness of space.

It was unlike anything he had experienced before. It was beautiful, so unlike the dying earth he knew. The ship turned automatically and headed toward the shining orb in front of him.

This was the first time he had seen New Blue from the outside. It was incredible, the same, and yet completely different from the earth that sat next to it. Earth was large and round, and was covered in thick, swirling tan clouds. Beyond that Silas could make out no defining features.

But New Blue One was different. There were thousands of small satellites orbiting around it, although Silas had no idea what they were for. Half of New Blue appeared to be completely metal, with large cavities cut from one side.

It looked something like an incomplete puzzle. Half metal, half a glorious replica of what earth used to be. But the problem was just that – it was a replica, not the actual thing.

Silas had been flying along for some time, and he had no idea where he was going. The Hilo was pre-programmed to the proper destination. This way nobody would ever get lost in space.

After he had settled the into steady travel, the plastic guards slowly released him, moving silently back inside their compartments. Silas decided to take advantage of the free time, he spread out in the seat, lying on a scattered mess of papers that had been blown around through the chaos.

Silas let his eyes close, and very soon he drifted off. Tired from everything that had happened since he left the cave, Silas welcomed sleep.

He had only been asleep for what felt like a few minutes, when a loud beeping noise woke him. He sat up quickly, and looked around through the windows of the Hilo craft.

He was definitely closer to New Blue. The lights inside the Hilo craft flashed madly as a soft female voice erupted from the speakers somewhere overhead.

"Please sit back. Initiating full speed mode." The voice drifted away as the beeping continued. Silas obeyed, sitting back in his seat.

He noticed then a piece of paper stuck to his cheek. He pulled it off and was about to toss it away when he noticed something written on it. It looked like a map. He turned it over and a note was scribbled on the back, it read:

Si, this is how you will find our friends. Please destroy this when you are done, we can't afford anyone finding it.

The rest of the page was blank. Silas turned it over again in his hands, completely shocked at his luck. The map looked to be hand-drawn, with a number of very complicated-looking diagrams scribbled along the outer edges. He was baffled by the note and more importantly, how he had found it. He hoped he could make more sense of it all when he arrived on New Blue.

He was stuffing the note in his pocket just as the plastic guard lowered over his head again. He watched it clamp securely around his chest, then he grabbed onto it firmly with both hands.

The number 10 appeared on the window directly in front of his face. He watched it curiously, wondering what it was.

Then, suddenly, it began counting backwards. He realized that it must be counting down to full speed mode. He gripped the guard tighter as it continued counting backwards past 4. When it reached 1 and then 0 he barely had a chance to prepare as he was thrown back into his seat again. Silas closed his eyes and tried to ignore the sudden crushing force against his body. It felt as though he might be ripped apart by the force alone.

Suddenly, the craft slowed, and he was thrown forward into the padded seat guard. Silas watched as the craft passed gracefully through the field of satellites.

Each satellite moved as he passed, politely allowing him access to the entrance of the planet. Then a hatch on the metal surface of New Blue opened up, and the craft flew right into it. It was extremely dark inside, but the craft knew where to go.

He could see thousands of metal rods holding up various parts of New Blue. As he entered the planet, Silas felt the side propellers start as a blast of oxygen hit the ship. The giant blades on top sat motionless – bent, and broken they would carry him no more.

Suddenly, a torrent of light made him temporarily blind. Silas waited for his eyes to focus as he squinted into the light ahead of him. Another hatch had opened, revealing a beautiful sky. He was flying up and out toward the surface of a city.

The Hilo craft was shaking slightly as the small propellers strained under the weight of the heavy ship. Silas could only hope the little blades would carry him as far as he needed to go.

He had no choice but to use the propellers when out in the oxygen saturated New Blue. The planet was beautiful in its own way, Silas thought – the grass was green, and perfectly trimmed.

Hundreds of new houses were scattered as far as he could see. It was an amazing site, and it had all been created by humankind. Silas felt amazed, and angry at the same time. He didn't know how to feel about the fake planet, and everything that it stood for.

The craft headed for another fenced-in landing pad, but this one appeared far less dangerous than the one on Earth. The security was minimal, and he had seen very few RT upon his arrival.

Silas held on to his seat as the craft began to hover over the landing pad, preparing for touchdown. Silas noticed that the launch pad was protected by a much smaller fence that did not cover the top. It was becoming more evident that the security on this planet was not as harsh as

Silas thought it would be.

He was trying to think of a way to escape the guards when the Hilo craft touched down on the landing pad, and the engines cut off. Two long metal robotic arms lowered onto either side of the craft and latched onto the small engines, relieving them of their duties.

The engines were sucked back into hatches on either side of the landing pad by the long arms, then the doors closed, leaving no sign that they had ever existed.

The doors unlocked, and Silas took a moment to observe his surroundings. The streets were strangely empty, and Silas found this fact odd – even as early in the day as it appeared.

Two brand-new Hilo crafts were gleaming across the landing pad, locked behind force fields. Silas knew there was no hope in stealing one of those. When he finally jumped out of the craft, Silas felt wobbly after his flight. He had to stop and steady himself before he continued.

Silas peaked around the Hilo craft to make sure it was clear before he ran toward the fence. Gathering his strength, he leaned back, and then pushing hard, leaping over the fence. His legs slammed into the pavement on the other side, sending a shock-wave through his bones.

The ground beneath his feet had crumbled slightly. Amazed he kicked over a piece of pavement with his foot. He started running along the rows of new houses. Silas ran until he heard the sound of someone talking, the sound made him slow to a normal speed.

He walked casually across the street, meeting a young couple on the sidewalk. They both looked at him as he walked by. He suddenly became aware of his appearance. He must have been very dirty, his clothes torn, and he was definitely covered in sweat from the run.

"What happened to you?" The boy said as he took in Silas' gnarled appearance.

Silas tried to think of something quickly as he glanced behind him to make sure he wasn't being followed.

"Gardening." He said as he spotted a bunch of flowers on someone's lawn.

But the girl must have recognized him – she turned to the boy and gave him a look that clearly expressed her concern. The boy turned to Silas again, his face full of fear.

"It's you." Was all he managed to say. Silas

considered what would happen if he had to kill the couple. But before he could think that far, the sound of sirens filled his ears so loudly that it sent him to his knees.

Pressing hard on his ears, Silas tried to block out the sound. He looked through his tear-filled eyes for the source of the noise.

He had barely caught a glimpse of his attackers, before he felt cool unconsciousness sweeping over him in waves. He tried desperately to focus, to stay in the moment, but the world faded fast as the sirens continued to blare.

TWENTY-FIVE

A soft pinging pricked his sensitive ears to life. Silas opened his eyes, allowing the dim light to flood in. It took him a moment to realize where he was, or even what was happening. Everything blurred together like a funny dream. All he knew for certain was that his head hurt. Slowly, his vision cleared and the room was revealed to him in hazy facets.

Silas was accustomed to seeing things as they were – his new eyes had shown him the world in great detail, more than any other man could ever see. But something about this room made it hard to focus. The strange dim lighting made his head hurt with more intensity.

The room was a perfect square, similar to his cell at the lab, but darker – the door was invisible. Silas noticed with a start as he looked down that his wrists were encased in a thick metal strap. The familiar red light blinked slowly across the silver band. He was in prison, the red light meaning *high security.*

Silas felt a dizzy sickness come over him. Lying his head back against the padded wall, he tried to stay focused – to figure a way out.

The sudden voice broke through his thoughts, and made him jump to his feet. Silas looked around, there was nobody there. In fact, the room around him was completely empty. But Silas was still on edge, the voice had sounded much too close.

"You really are more impressive in person." The slow voice spoke. Silas looked around for the source, but found nothing. "Don't be nervous now, we won't hurt you." Silas almost laughed at this. The very thought of a simple human harming his new body seemed pathetic.

"Who are you? Show your face!" Silas said as the anger twisted inside him.

"My name is none of your concern. *I am the chief of the Rescue Team.*" The voice spoke the last line particularly slow, as if he was extremely proud of that fact. Silas smirked at the man's arrogance.

"Too afraid to come in and talk face-to-face are you?" Silas's head throbbed, but he was certain the man would be no match for him.

"I'm not stupid. That is why they made me chief." The voice laughed harshly through the invisible speaker.

"Where am I?"

"New Blue Max Security Prison, that's where you are my friend, and you won't be leaving... *ever*."

Silas took this in; he had never liked being controlled by anything. Something about the chief's voice made Silas doubt his own self-control as the rage began to flood the back of his eyes.

"If you think you can keep me here, you are wrong." Silas said quietly, letting the full power of his voice take over. It was quiet for a moment before the man spoke again.

"We'll see." The room beeped. Silas knew the conversation was over, so he resumed his position against the padded wall. He smiled as the realization sunk in – getting out was going to be even easier than he thought. Silas took advantage of the comfortable prison cell, and enjoyed a good-nights rest.

***

The next morning, Silas got to work early. He was not going to waste any of his precious time, not when so many people were depending on him for their futures. Sleep had given him the fuel he needed, and Silas knew exactly what to do next.

He sat in the middle of the room holding his arm in front of him. He focused hard on the thick metal that twisted smoothly around his wrist. Breaking the metal would do no good, so instead he focused on the tiny flashing light.

Focusing all of his power into the red light, he contracted his mind around the source that fed the glow. Silas could feel the sweat building on his forehead as he worked. Suddenly, the light flashed frantically, and then it was gone.

Just as the light vanished from his bound wrists, the sound of sirens blasted through his cell. Five bodies slithered through the walls, each holding a shock stick. Silas smiled at them. He knew that they would not be able to hit him, not this time.

The first man swung, causing a cascading wall of identical attacks from his teammates. Silas dodged each attack with ease; it seemed like each one of the officers moved in slow motion. Silas landed his first kick on one man's throat. The officer gurgled once before he fell face down on the white floor.

Two more went down in the same fashion, but the last two ran at him, swinging their shock sticks through the air. Silas dodged and ripped the weapons from their hands so quickly their human eyes could not see.

The sudden angry surge building inside him sent his eyesight green. The green light reflected off the two men's horrified faces as Silas rushed them, slashing the shock sticks across their weak, unprotected chests.

Silas worked quickly, grabbing the wrist of the man lying nearest to him. He held it in his hand while picking up the man's left thumb and pressing it into the print slot on the his own wrist. The wristband beeped as the cuff released from the man's wrist.

Silas held the wristband firmly as he ran for the opposite wall, and for a moment the wall went crystal clear. He felt as though he was walking through a waterfall, then he appeared in a long and deserted hallway. Silas looked back to see a flat stone wall where his cell had been.

A golden plaque was mounted to the wall baring the words: *Special security cell: Please enter with caution.* Silas noticed several others that bore the same warning along the hallway.

As Silas ran from the hallway, he heard the frantic footsteps of officers hurrying down the stairs above him. But he had found what he was looking for, the staircase before him was clearly labeled: *Rescue Team Mechanic Systems Garage.*

It was exactly what he needed, and with a flash of inspiration, Silas hurried down the stairs as fast as his feet would carry him. He appeared at the bottom of the stairs breathing hard. His energy was draining fast and he needed to get out of the prison as quickly as possible.

Silas looked around the massive, high-ceiling garage until he found what he was looking for. A small demo craft sat gleaming in the sunlight of New Blue. Silas ran for craft, knowing he would have only seconds before the RT detected his presence.

Approaching the security door, Silas waved the wristband he had stolen in front of the sensor frantically. It beeped once, and then the door flew open smoothly, revealing the brilliant blue sky above.

Silas pulled the door of the ship open, and climbed inside. The interior was very much like the massive Hilo craft he had crashed into the landing pad and Silas felt confident about flying it.

Suddenly, Silas felt something wet trickling along the side of his arm. The pain came after the shock of seeing his own blood spilling onto the seat beside him. Silas felt his eyes widen, he had not heard his attacker approach.

The man standing in front of him held an empty crossbow in his hands as he smiled at Silas's terrified expression. Silas looked down again to see a long metal arrow protruding from his left arm – it had gone deep.

"I told you..." the man said walking toward him. "I said you couldn't leave, didn't I?" Silas recognized the voice, and felt a familiar rage building inside him.

His eyes still glowed faintly from his previous fight, but the man seemed to pay no attention to that fact. There was a clicking sound as the crossbow reloaded, the man raised it swiftly and shot.

Silas moved, but too late – the metal arrow protruding from his arm had snagged the fabric of the seat. The end of the arrow broke off from the force of his sudden dodge. The second arrow struck his shoulder. Silas cried out in pain, and fell from the craft onto the cement floor. The crossbow proved to be a much stronger weapon than he had anticipated.

"Now you see, don't you? Why we are superior – why we control this planet." The chief kicked Silas in the ribs, rolling him over onto his back.

"Things like you should not be allowed to live. That's why we left them on earth, those stupid people who are below our level. We had to weed out the bad ones." The man crouched next the Silas, his foul breath blowing through yellow teeth as he spoke.

"We could not allow the new world to be tainted by vermin like you. And I want you to know, right now, that you will never leave this prison. My face will be the last you ever see."

The man stood again and raised the crossbow. Silas watched the trigger bend down as if in slow motion – the tip of the arrow pointed toward his face.

Silas growled as he grabbed the man's leg and squeezed. He heard the bones crunch as the chief screamed in pain, dropping the crossbow to the floor.

Silas stood, his arm hanging loosely at his side. He walked over to the man who was still howling on the floor. The chief looked up, his face full of anger, fear, and pain. Silas tilted his head to look at the man, *deciding*.

In one movement, Silas swooped down and picked the man up by the neck with his good arm. The man's crumbled leg swung beneath his body as Silas eyed him. The arrogance had never left the chief's eyes, though he was clearly afraid, he refused to accept what was happening.

Silas suddenly realized that killing him would be useless. There were dozens ready to take his place, maybe more – each with the same distorted mind, a way of thinking engraved on their psyches. Silas threw the man to the ground, where he landed with a bone crushing splat.

Silas looked at him for a moment longer before he turned back to the craft. He wasted no time starting it up – the blades whirling through the air. Silas was already in the sky when the backup RT hurried into the garage. He was long gone before they had any chance of catching him.

Silas steered away to the eastern side of the city, not stopping for anything. He dove down into the opening outside the city. Half the ground was missing, which made it easy to disappear beneath the surface of the planet. Silas did not bother turning on the lights, he could see fine in the dark.

Occasionally, a beam of sunlight would blast through one of the cracks, causing him to go blind for a moment. Silas tried to recall the map in his mind. Thankfully his memory was sharp, though it was hard to find anything among the pipes – everything looked similar.

Finally, he recognized a uniquely shaped pipe which resembled the letter A. It was on the map, he had remembered seeing it.

With a jolt of excitement, he turned past the A pipe and went down a very narrow tube. He was zooming along so fast that he almost flew over the camp before he even noticed it was there. Beneath him several lights twinkled. When his eyes adjusted he saw quite a few tents had been built on a metal platform.

He forced the craft to slow, and then hovered for a minute, looking for a place to land. Below, there was a woman pointing at him, attracting the attention of others scattered about the platform. The people gazed up at the craft with worried looks on their dirty faces.

A tall woman ran through the crowd looking up

at him. Her eyes brightened as she motioned for everyone to move out of the way. Slowly, the crowd cleared and the woman signaled him to lower the craft onto the open space.

Silas worried for a moment that the platform would not hold the craft. But as he slowly touched down, the surface seemed absolutely stable. Silas cut off the engine.

He looked around at the people who watched him with wide eyes, and curious expressions. The tall woman walked up to the craft without hesitation, and slid open the door. She took in his appearance and smiled without a hint of fear. Only pure joy decorated her features as she began speaking.

"You must be Silas." He nodded his response, and she smiled even wider. "My name is Zera, welcome to our refugee camp."

TWENTY-SIX

Vadell woke several hours later, but sleep had done nothing for her exhaustion. So far she had been kidnapped, and brought to a strange refugee camp by a guy she had never met. The weirdest thing about it was – *Sam was involved in the whole thing.*

Vadell had almost been arrested while trying to board a Hilo lift back to earth, all to rescue Sam. But it was *Sam* that had rescued her. She turned over on her back and observed the dark ceiling of the tent. It looked exactly the same as it had during the previous night. Vadell assumed it must be morning, she felt as though she had been asleep for several hours.

Just then, someone burst through the tent flap. It was the black-haired man again, Silas. He didn't look at her when he crossed the room. His face was pale, and he looked exhausted.

"What's going on?" Vadell said loudly. He acted like he hadn't heard her. She stood and walked to him, crossing her arms. Though she felt a little afraid of him, she was determined not to show it.

He had started to walk toward the tent flap again when she darted in front of him, blocking his path. He looked at her with his swirling eyes. His pupils seemed to move faster when he was irritated.

"*Move*." He said in a slow, deadly voice. The sound of his voice was so frightening that she *almost* moved.

"I want to know what is going on." She said while trying to keep her voice strong.

"You will find out soon enough, now let me through." He picked her up with one arm and looked at her furiously. "I understand you are confused, but I have no time for this. There are things happening right now that are far more important than you." He was so close that she could feel his warm breath on her face – his eyes swirling dangerously.

He flung her casually with one arm across the room and onto her pillow bed. She landed hard, bouncing on the soft pillows.

By the time she scrambled to her feet he was already gone. The tent flap swaying was the only evidence he had even been there. Vadell marched out of the tent onto the torch-lit platform. She was determined not to be pushed around. She walked through the crowd of curious refugees without paying them the slightest attention.

Vadell had to know what was happening. Her best friend Lync was still being held captive by the RT. Vadell could not bring herself to think about what might have happened to Lync.

She spotted Silas on the other side of the platform, talking to a group of people – including the tall woman, and two men Vadell didn't know.

She marched right up to him and slammed her fist into his shoulder. It obviously did not hurt him, though she could hardly say the same for herself as she grabbed her fist in pain, rubbing her knuckles softly.

He turned to her slowly, and this time his face was livid. She cooled off immediately, fear replacing any anger she had toward him. Vadell backed away slowly and he stood completely still. The tall woman placed a thin-fingered hand on his muscular shoulder and he appeared to relax a little. Vadell turned and ran back to the tent, suddenly regretting her outburst.

She stopped when she neared her temporary

home, and looked at the small craft that had brought her to the platform. Three other small ships sat next to it. One she recognized was a Hilo craft – Vadell wondered if she could fly it.

Peeking around the edge of the tents to ensure she was not being watched, she rushed through the shadows between the canvases, trying to stay out of sight. When she reached the craft, she slid open the door quickly and climbed inside, keeping her head low as she closed the door.

Vadell hid in the dark compartment for a few minutes before she began searching around for the start button. It all seemed more complicated than she thought.

Finally, she spotted the small ignition button, and reached out a petite pale hand to push it. But before she had even made it half-way, the door slid open and a pair of strong arms jerked her from her seat.

Silas was holding her at least a foot from the ground. He was much taller than she was, and his arms held her weight like she was nothing.

She squirmed in his grasp, fear overcoming her. He must have noticed this because his eyes softened a little, and he sighed.

"Why can't you just behave?" His voice sounded a little amused.

She looked at him meekly. "I just want to help my friend, OK. I told you she was captured." Vadell managed to get the words out in a small cracked voice. Silas sat her on her feet gently, a hint of sadness in his swirling eyes.

"I understand that you want to help your friend, but that is not the place for you – you could be captured. Do you know what I would have to do to get you back?" He looked at her seriously, but his eyes were still gentle.

"Then tell me what you need me for, what Sam needs me for." He looked at her for a long time, deciding what to say.

"Sam says you are pretty smart, so that is useful to me. And I promised him I would find you and bring you back to the cave." He said, and then clearly noticed he had said too much.

"The cave?" Vadell said quietly, speaking only to Silas.

"You will see for yourself when we get there. I can't trust anyone, not even *here*." He looked at her for a moment longer, and then turned his back to her, skulking back into one of the bigger tents.

Everyone was quiet as they watched her walk by. Trying to run away had been a stupid idea. She had drawn unwanted attention to herself. Vadell was afraid of Silas, but she was even more afraid for Lync. What would the RT do to her?

Vadell had not even noticed that she was standing still until Silas appeared at the entrance of his tent, staring at her. He raised his hand, and motioned with his finger for her to follow him.

Vadell wasted no time rushing toward the massive tent. She didn't want to see any of them, their eyes watching her – waiting for her to act out again. She pushed through the tent and Silas was lying on the floor. His arms were folded behind his head as he peered up at the ceiling.

"I'll tell you, if you promise not to cause me any more trouble. When I give you an order, I expect you to follow it." He spoke slowly, his voice tired but serious. Vadell didn't like the idea of being bossed around, but she wouldn't dare argue with him. She *did* want to know what was happening, and the fact that he was willing to tell her was worth it.

"I Promise." She said. He twitched uncomfortably as she spoke, though Vadell could not understand the reason behind it.

Vadell crossed the room and sat down beside Silas on one of the fluffy pillows.

"The war is about to start, whether we are ready for it or not. The government of sector one back on earth is about to be attacked by a lab of rebels, who have been transformed..." He stopped and took a deep breath before continuing. "Into monsters like me."

It sounded to Vadell like he had planned exactly what to say to her. Perhaps he had said it so much in his mind that it was beginning to sound rehearsed.

"But what *are* you?" Vadell asked looking at the muscled gray-colored skin on his arm.

He sighed, adjusting his hands under his head. "I guess you could say I have been enhanced." He said casually. "The point is, a fight is about to break out between the government and about one-hundred mutants."

Vadell looked at him. She could only imagine what something like that would be capable of. The way he had tossed her across the room like she weighed two pounds, was enough to make her fear him.

"And what are you planning to do about it?"

Vadell asked.

"We can't really do anything. We are trying to move the refugees to the cave before it starts."

"But what is the cave!?" She said, fighting to keep her voice low. He turned his head to the side and looked at her, a simple reminder of their agreement. She closed her mouth, and he turned his eyes back to the ceiling.

"Your Sam is there, and that is all you need to know, at least for now."

"So when can we move?" She said seriously.

"The first team is leaving in about an hour, with Zera."

"But I don't understand how this could work. If the battle is happening on earth, then why would we be going there?" Silas sighed again. Vadell noticed the muscles in his arms flex.

"Yes we are going to earth, but we won't be staying there. We have a refuge there, a safe place. Once we all get there, we won't be coming back." He was quiet then, and Vadell didn't want to ask any more questions, she just wanted to be safe with Sam, Lync, and her family. Suddenly, her brain jolted.

"What about my family!?" She asked

frantically. "I can just leave and not come back. I have to bring them too."

Silas sat up and looked at her. "We have already sent for your mother and father. We don't separate families." He looked down at his hands and then back at her. "But I'm warning you, this will not be safe, or easy. There is no guarantee that we will all make it alive." Vadell could tell he was serious, and she considered this before she answered.

"I know." She said slowly. Silas nodded.

He stood up. "Come on then, we have work to do." Vadell just looked at him curiously. She couldn't imagine that he wanted her help. He seemed to know exactly what she was thinking, because he looked at her and smiled.

"Yes, I mean you. I can't go looking for your friend alone. I know the prison, but I don't know who I am looking for."

Vadell stood slowly, unbelieving. "Um, OK." She mumbled. He gave her a look that could only mean a repressed eye roll, then turned and walked out of the tent.

She followed him quickly, having to jog to keep up. He nodded to a few of the refugees as they passed, each nodding in turn as if exchanging some secret code that Vadell didn't understand.

Silas marched to a row of weapons, and extracted a small handgun from the line. He stuffed it neatly in the back pocket of his jeans, then he turned and grabbed a bag from a hook near the tent entrance.

Vadell followed him closely, fearing that he might change his mind and refuse to let her come along. He motioned for her to get into the craft, and so she did, climbing into the passenger seat without a second thought. She nearly fell clumsily, but somehow she managed to wedge herself between the door and the seat.

When she was finally inside, she watched Silas speak with the tall woman named Zera. The woman hugged him and whispered something in his ear. Afterward, he turned and jumped into the driver's seat.

"They are moving out in a few minutes, and once we have your friend, so will we." He said as he started the craft. They were in the air before she knew it, soaring through the silky darkness.

"You mean we're going to the cave *now*?" Vadell said vociferously. She could not believe they would be moving so soon. "What about my parents?"

"They are already being transported. Now stop asking questions." Vadell wanted to keep her promise to him, but she could hardly believe that her parents were already being moved to a place she was not certain even existed.

But Vadell remained quiet as they soared over NB1. In the brightness of the crystal clear sky, Vadell felt a sudden grip of fear. She had no idea how they could possibly rescue Lync.

The RT could make for a powerful enemy. She wondered if Silas had enough inhuman strength to free Lync from her prison, and still get them out alive.

But Silas had said that he knew the prison, he must have been there before, Vadell thought. *And what if he had escaped?* This idea made her fear him even more. She could not imagine how he had escaped such a high security place with his life intact.

The craft rumbled around her as it slowed, bringing her mind back to the present. Silas was focusing on something far ahead, but Vadell could see only blurry patches of land.

She had never seen anything so spectacular.

NB1 looked much better from the air. The plastic grass looked almost real.

"When we touch down you need to stay with me at all times." Silas's voice revealed no fear, but Vadell thought she heard sadness there instead.

"Yes, of course." She said in a small voice.

"I don't know what is going to happen to us, *to me...*" He paused, keeping his eyes on the ground below them. "But, no matter what, you have to follow my orders." He looked at her then, his eyes swirling. "You have to."

Vadell didn't know what to say. They watched each other for a moment, both knowing that the end could come for either of them at any time.

Her voice seemed to be stuck in her throat. She managed a small nod, and then looked away. The realization of what was coming churned inside her – writing like a snake in a raptor's talons.

Neither of them said a word as the prison came into view. The tall, vast building extended on forever beneath the humming Hilo craft. Silas stretched his gray fingers to the control panel where he pressed a small rectangular button. Instantly, the craft shot forward, engines roaring.

Vadell dug her fingers into the fabric of the

seat and gritted her teeth. Silas handled the craft like a professional, narrowly avoiding blurred objects in their path. He wound around the curved streets with ease.

Finally, he brought the Hilo to a stop exactly one block from the prison, where they landed with a loud plunk. He cut off the engine as soon as they touched down. Vadell was still gripping the seat fiercely when Silas grabbed his bag from the below the seat.

"Are you ready?" He turned to her, the same feeling of doom erupted between them.

Vadell wondered if she would ever see Sam again. She hesitated for a moment before she answered, knowing she wasn't ready. But would she ever be ready for what she had to do?

She bit her lip and looked out the window, the streets she knew so well sat clean, and uncluttered before her. She would never see these streets again – not after today.

"I'm ready." She said, taking in a deep breath and wondering if it would be among her last.

Silas jumped out of the craft, and Vadell tried her best to follow as they jogged toward an empty building near the prison.

When they approached the door, there was nobody in sight. Vadell heard a quick snap as the door swung open. It was dark inside, and she could only see the outline of Silas as she walked cautiously behind him.

Another crack set the room blazing with sunlight. Vadell looked around nervously for the source of light. Silas had ripped open a door near the staircase, and light flooded in, splashing across the dark floor, and over the empty space to land on the opposite wall where it settled.

Vadell followed Silas up the narrow winding staircase onto an empty landing. She wondered what this house had been built for. She was sure the neighboring prison would not be a perk for new home buyers. But then again, nobody really *chose* their home on NB1.

"What now?" Vadell asked as she watched Silas search the ceiling with his eyes.

The landing was empty, leading off into one solitary bedroom that also appeared vacant. Silas did not answer, but walked suddenly to the end of the landing where he leaped from the ground, scraping his fingers across the white, spotless ceiling. Suddenly, a blue square appeared above his head. Flashing slowly, the light became brighter as she watched in amazement.

"Open." Silas said confidently. The blue square immediately turned transparent, and then vanished all together.

Vadell was just about to ask what was happening, when a snake slithered from the opening. She screamed and flew against the wall. Silas stood watching as another snake glided slowly onto the floor.

Vadell expected them to fall, but they merely hung there, resting their heads on the smooth floor – they seemed to be hanging from their tales.

Silas approached them, and gradually the two snakes went rigid. Steps appeared between the bodies of the snakes. It was a ladder, Vadell realized with a start. *The snakes formed a ladder to the attic!*

"Show-offs." She mumbled as she walked toward the hissing ladder. "This is safe right?" She asked when Silas moved to take his first step.

"I think so." He placed one foot on the first step. He must have been satisfied, because he gripped the two snakes then and began to climb.

"This is just a test house you know..." Vadell yelled up at him as he pulled himself safely onto

BRITTNEY STEWART

the attic floor. Silas leaned over and gave her a look that could have melted her face off.

Vadell ignored him and began her ascent. One of the snakes hissed violently as she climbed, speeding up her pace considerably. Impatient sighs flowed from somewhere above.

The attic was dark, but a small stream of light came from behind a thick curtain near the end of the room. Silas pulled her safely to the attic, where she moved swiftly away from the snake ladder into yet another empty room.

"Hurry." Silas whispered as he crossed the room and ripped the curtains from the window with a wave of his arm.

But the window was not a window at all; it was a massive glass door leading onto a small balcony. Vadell hurried to Silas's side, and peered through the glass. The balcony overlooked the prison. Vadell could think of no good reason why anyone would want to sit and look at a prison all day.

"What are we going to do?" Vadell asked.

"What do you see out there?" Silas replied with a snigger. Vadell had never heard him laugh before, and the sound seemed to lighten the room.

"Well, I see the prison roof... And, well, that's about it." It hit her just after she said it – *the roof.*

"But how?" She wondered more to herself than to Silas.

Silas looked at her stunned. He clearly thought she would have figured out the answer to this question already.

"Oh no." Vadell said sharply, looking from the balcony to the prison roof. "We can't jump! It's at least thirty feet!"

"That's no problem for me." Silas grinned.

"You can't possibly! The fence is electrified, if we fell..." Silas grabbed her around the waist without warning, tossing her gently onto his muscled shoulder.

Vadell wanted to object, but she remembered her promise. She settled onto his shoulder, grabbing two fistfuls of his dirty white t-shirt. Silas held her in place with one arm while the other pulled them both to the edge of the balcony.

Vadell surveyed the ground beneath them. She felt her stomach flip – Silas was balancing on the guardrails of the terrace. Vadell heard him take a deep breath, and the thought passed through her mind that perhaps she should close her eyes. But it was too late, he had already pushed off from the railing, sending them both rocketing into the sky.

Up and over the fence they flew as Silas angled his body toward the prison's rooftop. Vadell held on as tightly as she could, digging her fingers into his back. They began to fall down toward the roof. The descent made her stomach do a somersault.

They landed hard on the roof, the impact shaking her joints loose from their sockets. Silas sat her on her feet in front of him. It took her a few minutes to get her bearings.

"You alright?" He smiled again, his white teeth only a few inches from her. She felt a curious sensation creep into her stomach, and she was certain it had nothing to do with the acrobatics.

"Um, fine." she mumbled still gazing transfixed at his intimidating features.

She had never seen him smile before. The prospect of jumping onto the prison rooftop had brought about a different side of him, a less frightening, more carefree side.

Silas looked at her curiously for a moment before turning to take in the deserted rooftop. She followed him slowly. The roof seemed like any other rooftop, somehow she had imagined it being more high-tech. Silas pulled out his hand gun, and motioned for her. She obeyed immediately, kneeling beside him.

"In five seconds, twelve guards are going to appear on this rooftop. I want you to hide behind this metal frame. Don't come out until I tell you to."

Vadell suddenly felt very nervous. "But why? How do they know we are here?" Vadell swallowed at the lump in her throat.

"Motion sensors." He said as if this were obvious. "Just stay here, OK?" His voice going back to the inhuman one, the one that could make her shake with fear.

"I will." She whispered as the sound of a dozen footsteps approached.

Vadell soared behind the metal framing. She watched through the cracks as Silas turned at lightning speed and flew at the group of armed guards. There was nothing she could do to help as she watched Silas blur into a flash of color around the confused guards, who began firing at anything that moved.

Bullets and darts bounced off every surface of the rooftop. Vadell ducked to avoid a stray arrow that ricocheted off the metal, and landed in front of her. One by one the men fell, each howling in pain.

In a matter of minutes, each officer lie motionless on the ground. Vadell wondered if they were still alive as she watched Silas sort through their weapons, putting several in his bag.

"Hurry, let's move." He shouted at her and she obeyed. Crawling from her hiding place, she jogged to catch up to him.

"Stay close." he said, as they came through the open door where the officers had just entered. Once inside, Vadell heard the ringing chime of an alarm shoot through the building. The motion sensors had alerted the whole building of their intrusion.

Vadell moved closer to Silas who was leading her down a long, artificially-lit hallway. They came to a doorway that was clearly locked.

Silas extracted a bracelet from his bag, and swung it in front of the security sensor. It beeped once and then the door slid open, revealing a small, ordinary room with rows of cabinets. Vadell watched as Silas searched for an unknown object.

He obviously had planned his attack on the prison well.

Running his bracelet across a locked cabinet, it beeped once. From the depths of the cabinet Silas pulled out two more bracelets, but these were not the same as the one he held in his hand. These were smaller, each with a small blinking green light.

Silas walked across the room and grabbed her wrist. Vadell hadn't noticed before how hot his skin felt. He clamped the bracelet firmly to her wrists, and did the same to his own.

"Hurry, we are running out of time." He urged as he ran into the hall again.

Vadell stayed close as they twisted through the many hallways of the prison. Each one lined with golden plaques. Vadell had never seen the inside before, not even the news stations were allowed to broadcast from the inside, since it was considered top-secret.

Finally, they found the hallway they had been looking for. It was the women's section of the prison. But finding Lync among the rows of invisible doors seemed like an impossible task.

Just when her worries began to set in, Silas

stepped forward into the middle of the hall. He held his hands to the sky as if feeling the air for some sign that would show him the way.

His eyes were closed, and Vadell made no sound for fear of breaking his concentration – though what exactly he was concentrating on she could not fathom.

Unexpectedly, the sound of footsteps reverberated off the walls of the hallway into the empty women's sector where Vadell stood watching Silas. She panicked, wondering what to do, wondering if he had heard the footsteps.

Silas turned suddenly, moving so quickly that Vadell could not believe her own eyes. They were flying across the room. Vadell was suspended in the air by his massive arm as they soared into one of the invisible doorways.

They landed on a soft padded surface. Vadell raised her head to take in the room. It was small, about the size of her bedroom at home, but the ceiling was vast.

It took her a moment to recognize that Silas was not the only other person in the room. A small figure was cowering in the corner, her face hidden behind a curtain of light brown hair.

Vadell's heart leaped, she ran to the figure –
crouching down beside the tiny, shaking form of
her best friend.

TWENTY-SEVEN

The two of them stared at each other, Lync's eyes were wide. She looked shocked, but also distant, as if she questioned reality.

"It's me. Lync we have to go." Vadell whispered as Lync stared, her face confused. But Lync was not looking at her anymore. She was staring behind Vadell, where Silas was waiting.

"It's him." Lync whispered, her face suddenly flashing with fear. She backed into the wall, pressing herself as far away from him as she could manage.

"It's OK, he is here to help us. He helped me find you." Vadell encouraged. Lync stood then and Vadell followed cautiously, looking between the two of them.

"But he isn't human." Lync said, never taking her eyes off Silas – she did not rust him. Silas looked down at his feet. Vadell felt as if Silas had known this would happen.

"And you think the people keeping you here

are any more human than he is?" Vadell said feeling frustrated at her friend. "This man *saved* my life Lync. I would trust him before anyone in this place." And she meant it – Silas had proven himself. Everything he did, he did because he was trying to save them.

"We should hurry, they will find us soon." Lync said, still looking at Silas suspiciously. He walked forward, extending his bracelet to hers, but she stepped back.

"You do it." Lync ordered Vadell, who didn't understand what she was supposed to be doing. "Scan my bracelet with yours." Lync said.

Vadell hesitated, and then moved forward, pressing her bracelet against Lync's. The bracelet around Lyncs arm flashed from red, to orange and then to green.

"We have to go." Silas said, and his deep voice seemed to fill the small room with electricity. Lync nodded and Vadell walked forward to join him. The three of them ran quietly back to the roof.

Vadell fought a mixture of emotions as they struggled up the staircase. She was more than happy to have Lync with them, alive, and virtually unharmed. But the tension between Lync and Silas was staggering.

The fact that Lync did not trust him would make things difficult. They needed to work as one if all of them were going to make it out alive. But Vadell doubted Lync would allow Silas to order her around.

When they made it to the rooftop, the scene was much worse than Vadell had anticipated. At least fifty prison guards were waiting on them, guns raised. Silas's face was completely calm as he surveyed the troop in front of him.

Suddenly, a man stepped from the ranks and walked forward, stopping two feet from Silas. The two stared at each other as if exchanging some mental conversation. Then the man spoke.

"I had hoped you would come back. We had fun last time, didn't we." The man tapped his leg where he wore a thick plastic brace. He sniggered, but did not move any closer.

"What can I say, I missed you." Silas said. Vadell could not understand why the RT had not attacked yet.

"You won't be escaping this time. The garage is on lock down, you can't leave New Blue." The man smiled, crinkling the corners of his small beady eyes. Silas's fists tightened, and Vadell prepared for the worst.

"You know I won't stay here willingly, anyone who wants to try and keep me here will die. I promise you." Silas's voice was deadly. Vadell was shocked when the man only laughed at him. She grabbed Lync's arm when she saw Silas's eyes twitch toward a metal pole protruding from the rooftop.

It all happened at once – the snapping of metal, and the sickening sound as the metal pole was thrust through the man's abdomen. His laughter died out when he noticed what had happened. Falling backward several men behind him stepped forward to catch him, while the rest raised their guns.

Suddenly, a bright green light shot from Silas and cast a glow upon the guards. It took Vadell a few seconds to realize that the light was emitting from Silas's eyes. The RT looked shocked, their faces bathed in green, but none backed away. They stood bolted to the spot, ready to fire.

Then Vadell heard something in the distance – a high pitched noise that she had never heard before. It seemed to be coming from all around them. Silas raised his hands to the sky, and the noise stopped, everything went quiet. Then a massive shock wave hit them all. With a loud bang, each one of the guards tumbled off the edge of the roof, falling three stories to the hard ground below.

Even though it had not been directed at them, the explosion knocked Vadell and Lync backwards onto the rooftop. They lie there waiting for the ground to stop shaking. Silas seemed to be shaking with the resulting earthquake. His previously strong frame looked feeble as he stumbled toward them.

"Hurry." He held his hands out to them.

Lync looked frightened, but took his hand anyway. Silas pulled them to their feet, and then lifted Lync to his back. He did the same with Vadell, pinning them both to his shoulders.

Vadell noticed his arms were shaking. She worried that he would not be able to make the jump. Silas was breathing hard as he ran full-speed toward the edge of the roof.

Vadell suppressed a scream as the rooftop disappeared from beneath them – revealing the plastic grass below, and the powerful electric fence. Vadell had a horrible image in her mind, the three of them falling into the fence and never making it off the planet.

But she pushed the thought away, and held on tighter to Silas. With a bone crunching thud, the three landed on the balcony. The impact sent Lync and Vadell flying into the attic as Silas rolled into the wall where he lie on the floor, unmoving. The darkening sky made it hard to see as Vadell stumbled toward him.

"We have to get him up!" Vadell cried, pulling his arm. He was heavier than she could have ever imagined. She tugged with all her strength, but he barely moved. Though his eyes were closed, Vadell could still see the green glow from behind his eyelids. *He was alive.*

"We have to go V!" Lync yelled pointing out the window toward the prison. Several more guards had made it to the roof, and even more were on the ground.

The sound of patrol sirens filled the small room, Vadell panicked, pulling harder on Silas's arm. His eyes fluttered – she held her breath.

He stood up so quickly that it almost pulled her arm from the socket. She was still gripping his forearm with both hands. He looked at her, exhausted – his swirling eyes were still tinted with the green light that seemed to be coming from somewhere inside him. Vadell buried herself in his chest, she felt him tense before he broke the hug. Pulling away he held her by her shoulders in front of him, breathing hard.

"We have to go to the control port..." He took another deep breath, and then continued. "That is the only way we are going to get off this planet."

"Well, then let's go!" Lync yelled again, hurrying toward the exit.

When they had all made it down the snake ladder, the two of them followed an exhausted Silas out onto the street where the Hilo craft sat shadowed by twilight.

They were in the air before the patrol cars came into view. They soared to the opposite side of the city, to a massive five story control station that stood at the edge, where the earth ended and the forest of metal began.

Vadell sat next to Silas watching his every move – his eyelids lowered over his swirling green-tinted eyes. He had very little energy, and she could only hope that they would make it to the control station in time. It wasn't until they landed that Vadell noticed a small trickle of blood running down the back of Silas's neck.

"Your head." Vadell whispered, and Silas ran his

hand down the back of his black hair. His hand returned covered in deep red blood. They both looked at each other. Silas looked pale, his gray skin turning a chalky white.

"I must have hit it on the jump" He said weakly.

"You can't go in there." Vadell said.

"Of course I can, and I will." He said, using his most convincing voice. Vadell knew better.

"You won't make it. If you go, then we will be caught trying to get you out..."

"I could do it. I could open the hatch and be back here before you know I'm gone." Lync said quickly, scanning the control station for guards with her deep blue eyes.

Silas seemed to be having some internal struggle, and then he nodded. Too weak to speak, he collapsed back in his seat, fighting to hold his eyes open.

Lync and Vadell snuck in through the back security gate, Lync had no trouble decoding the lock, so the entrance was easy enough. It was only by some miracle though, that they did not meet any guards on their way to the top of the control station. The entire staircase was made of iron. The climb was steep, but surrounded by rails, which Vadell held tightly to as they climbed for what felt like hours. Vadell hoped that the craft would not be seen, she doubted Silas had any fight left in him, and without him, they would be lost.

When they made it to the top of the control center, Vadell pulled Lync to a stop just around the corner from the main entrance. Two guards stood outside the doors of the control room. Vadell felt her heart drop, the guards were armed. Out of nowhere, Lync pulled a silencer from her pocket and held it toward the guards with her small hands.

"Where did you get that?" Vadell whispered. Lync just smiled.

"I took it from your mutant friend." She said as she aimed the gun toward the guard nearest to the door.

"Be careful, you don't know how to..." But it was too late, Lync had shot the first guard, and the second before he had time to react. Lync smiled to herself again.

"Those guys are going to be so sore in the morning." She giggled, but Vadell did not find it funny. She hurried for the door, letting Lync go first. She cracked it open, and Lync motioned for her to come inside.

The room was gigantic, and filled with computers. Half of the room was made of glass, allowing for a perfect view of NB1's exit hatches. They approached the main control panel and Lync looked it over curiously.

"I think this one..." She pointed to a button with a giant letter 4 on it. "I think that is the one we want." Lync glanced out toward the dimly lit hatches, and then returned her attention to the control panel where she reached for number 4 – pressing it cautiously. Both of them held their breath as they waited for some sign that it had, or had not worked.

The room was devoured by flashing lights – sirens blasted their ears. They both panicked, looking from the windows Vadell saw the hatch swing open.

Bolting for the door, they hurried past the unconscious guards, and down the steep stairs. The sirens continued, but even through the blasting racket Vadell could hear the sound of footsteps coming from someplace high above. They only had a few minutes to escape before the RT would catch up with them.

Two flights of stairs from the bottom, a

piercing scream made Vadell stop in her tracks. She glanced behind her and was shocked to see several men coming down the stairs, and to her horror, Lync's limp body tumbling down toward the railing.

"Lync!" Vadell yelled without thinking, alerting the men who looked up. One shouted something, and then two came racing down the stairs, stepping over Lync as they hurried toward her.

Suddenly, one of them fell forward, the sound of his face hitting the iron echoed down the stairs. Lync was crawling away from her predators, and Vadell wanted desperately to help her, but the second guard was gaining on her.

"Run V!" Lync shouted down the stairs. Vadell ducked as the guard aimed for her head, the bullet zoomed past her skull, missing it by inches.

Vadell was torn between rescuing Lync, and saving Silas. Sam's face came into her mind, and the horrible thought of never seeing him again stabbed her in the chest.

Vadell whirled around and ran up the stairs toward Lync. The man shot at her again, and Vadell dropped, covering her head. The bullet bounced off the metal with a clang, missing her.

"Aaaaaaaah!" Lync's scream traveled through the stairwell. Vadell looked up just in time to see another guard standing behind where Lync had been lying.

In an instant the man had pushed Lync under the railing, sending her flying from the edge of the stairs – landing somewhere two floors below. Vadell could still hear screaming, and then she noticed it was her own scream that echoed around her.

She screamed for her friend, for a response, a sign of life. But Vadell knew it was over. *Lync was gone.* In a flash of anger, and despair she flew down the stairs, leaping over the last few steps before bursting through the exit, and out into the open air.

Her heart pounded in her ears drums, her eyes were blinded by tears. She ran for the Hilo craft as quickly as she could, her legs wobbling beneath her as her stomach flipped.

She wrenched open the door to the craft, and flung herself inside. The guards would not be far behind so she wasted no time pulling the door shut behind her. Silas was slumped in his seat, eyes closed. Vadell punched him hard on the arm, but he remained motionless, his lungs moving his strong chest to rise and fall.

"WAKE UP!" She screamed at him. "PLEASE! WAKE UP!" She pounded her fist into his arm again, feeling the pain as her knuckles bruised. But the pain was nothing compared to what she felt inside. The agony of a lost friend devastated every corner of her mind and body.

Suddenly, his eyes fluttered, and slowly fell open. "We have to go hurry!" Vadell yelled at him as the bullets bounced off the metal craft.

He sat up straight and looked at her, clearly noticing Lync's absence. Vadell just shook her head, tears streaming down her face and into her lap. Silas clenched his jaw, and started the engine, steering them up to the open hatch.

Flashing lights gathered in the distance as the patrol cars appeared. Silas hit full speed, sending them flying through their exit. The first door closed behind them, and then a second hatch began to close.

Silas squeezed the ship through the closing hatch just in time. The shriek of metal on metal sent a ringing sound through Vadell's ears.

"It has one of the engines!" Silas yelled as he pushed the ship further. A snapping sound told them they were free, as they soared into space. Vadell looked back at the hatch and noticed the small engine caught between the doors, pinning it open.

"Oh..." Silas said before the sound of a thunderous explosion blasted them forward and down toward earth's surface. Debris flew with them like rain from space. Giant pieces of metal had dislodged from NB1 and were beginning to fly toward earth.

The impact was incredible, shaking them in their seats as they plummeted to earth's surface. The small propellers kicked in when they entered the atmosphere, slowing them down dramatically. Silas steered carefully, trying to avoid the debris from NB1.

Hundreds of fallen pieces showered around them, narrowly missing their ship. Silas sped up again, blasting them to the ground with incredibly speed.

As soon as they touched down on the empty plains Silas grabbed Vadell by the arm, yanking her from her seat as the debris continued falling around them. Silas carried her and ran, the impact of his footfalls jarring her bones.

They headed for the trees ahead, and Vadell

wondered where they were going, how they could possibly get away. Suddenly, the sound of engines roaring exploded in her ears, a ship was coming, not one, but several, and in all directions. Silas had stopped running, and was looking up at the nearest of the ships that lowered onto the dusty plains.

"Si!" A female voice yelled over the sound of the landing ships. Several people came out of the craft, rushing toward them.

"Terra! You have to get the girl out of here, take her back to the cave!" Silas spoke, his voice strained with exhaustion.

"I'm not leaving you here." Terra said looking up at the ships now approaching. "They're coming Si, they were waiting on you."

"We can take her." Came another voice from behind Terra. An old man stood there, what was left of his hair waved with the wind thrown from the propellers. They looked at each other, and nodded.

"Go, I'll be there when this is done." Silas glanced at Vadell, and she felt a terrible sadness grip her. She wanted him to survive more than anything, and she could not understand why – she barely knew him.

Vadell allowed herself one last glance before she stepped onto the ship – one last look at the man who would save the world. He was the last of a dying race, the last of the true heroes. Not because of his abilities, but because of spirit.

Vadell could see that part of him in the moments before she boarded the craft. He would give everything to save the innocent, and Vadell was positive that he would reach for that goal until his end.

TWENTY-EIGHT

The ground rumbled beneath their feet as they watched the craft ascend into the air – headed for the safety its occupants deserved. Silas recalled, while Terra stood beside him, why he had done it all.

It was because they *deserved* it. Those people who had been deemed unworthy by the government, and left to die, they were the only ones who deserved to live. Terra's small hand wound around his as they watched two more ships close in on them.

"We can't stop this." She said over the roar of the engines.

"We can try." He squeezed her hand, studying her sad face. Once again their hearts seemed to beat together, her face revealing the pain he felt.

Terra turned to Silas, and closed the distance between them in one step. The kiss lasted forever, and for only an instant. All of the things unsaid and the broken promises faded away, mending themselves. Silas wanted to say so much, but there was nothing that had not already been said.

The first ship touched down, shaking the ground and breaking them apart. He looked at her, knowing they felt the same. Her face turned toward the ship as they walked hand-in-hand to face the enemy.

"Silas!" A rough voice called over the growling engines. Silas recognized it at once, but when he looked up he was shocked. He had been expecting the doctor, expecting his chubby frame, his gnarled teeth, and bespectacled eyes.

But the creature before him was none of what he remembered. Instead he was massive, his muscular arms rippled as he walked toward them. He no longer wore glasses, and as he smiled Silas noticed his yellowing, crooked teeth had been filed into sharp points.

"I thought I had lost you forever." His voice was deep and rough as he spoke the words of a lost lover, twisted into something different.

He stood before them changed, changed into a monster worse than anything Silas had imagined. The second ship landed, and several more mutants stepped out. They all resembled him, their skin a dull gray-brown, their muscles clearly visible.

They walked forward with arrogant expressions as they filed in behind the doctor.

"I will waste no more time here." He said wickedly. "I'll make it simple, either you come back and join our ranks, or we kill you."

Silas raised his eyebrow. "You honestly think I'm coming back? You don't even understand what you are doing!" Silas yelled pushing Terra slightly behind him.

"Oh, I know exactly what I'm doing, Silas." He paused gesturing toward one of his creations. "I've worked out all the kinks. They are stronger than you. You won't win this battle." Silas wondered fleetingly if the doctor was right, if the new enemies were too strong to fight.

"No." He paused glaring at the doctor. "I won't help you destroy the new government. I've found my place, now leave us alone." Silas stared at the doctor, who returned his gaze steadily. They were sizing each other up – each determining their odds for victory.

Suddenly, the doctor made a move, pulling a massive sword from his belt, and slashing the air once. Silas barely had time react as the doctor charged him.

Just as Silas moved to dodge the blow, a gurgling sound filled the air, and everything went quiet around him. He looked down to examine his wound, and found that he had none, instead a crumpled body lie at his feet, holding desperately to his ankle.

Terra was dying before his eyes; the sword protruding from her stomach had been the fatal blow. Silas fell beside her, the anger and sadness boiling red-hot inside of him. Silas forgot about the doctor, about the army, and about the war.

Terra looked at him through blood and tears. Through their connected hearts he could feel her fading away. He wanted desperately to save her, but his powers could do nothing. He held her hand as he watched her wither. It all seemed unfair to him, the years they had wasted, the time they had lost because of a dying world.

She smiled at him, his favorite smile. The tears burned in his eyes, and reflected in hers. He listened as her heartbeat faded. In that moment the old Silas – the human part of him died with her.

Her life had been the one thing keeping him in control, but she was gone, and so was his humanity. Silas stood, giving himself over to the rage, and the agony. The doctor looked at him, ready to test his strength. He anticipated the battle with excitement, and Silas anticipated the kill.

Just as Silas tightened his muscles to attack, another ship landed with a thundering boom. The ground shook beneath them as another ship landed, and then another.

Silas saw in the distance a man step out, followed by at least fifty more. Through his excellent vision, Silas saw for the first time, *hope.*

Franklin stood at the front of the battle, his hand held high, behind him were more recruits, more mutations, but this time they would not be fighting against him.

The roar of the two armies shook the ground and as they charged forward, running at lightning speed. Each of them held no weapon – they were the weapons. Silas wasted no time, he leaped onto the doctor, sending them both tumbling to the sandy ground.

A piece of twisted metal flew from the sky, and Silas moved to dodge it. His enemy followed, missing the jagged spike by inches. The doctor pulled out a small knife, slashing Silas across the chest.

The doctor was quick, sending the blade across his neck before he could react. Blood spurted across the ground, soaking his shirt. Silas clutched his throat with his free hand, and planted a kick into the doctor's chest. The doctor gasped as he fell back crashing into the earth, the blade flying from his hand.

The air was filled with the sounds of war as the two armies collided. The doctor's army was greatly outnumbered by Franklin's army of recruits. Silas felt like victory was in reach for the first time in months.

Another massive piece of metal flew from the sky in the form of a flaming fireball, it landed deep into the earth causing a shock wave after it.

The feeble earth cracked, and fell into nothing. A thin jagged canyon appeared where the earth had been. Silas had seen this all before, and he recognized frightfully, the canyon of his dream. He had been thrown over the edge to die by an enormous red-eyed monster.

The doctor came at him again, and he dodged the flying kick by inches. Suddenly, his eyes were shrouded in a green haze. The doctor slammed his fist into Silas's face, causing him to fly backward and land near the canyon's edge.

The pain shook him like nothing he had felt before. He had grown accustomed to fighting, but never with someone of the same strength.

Silas gathered himself to his feet, feeling angrier than ever. He turned to the doctor, and they faced each other for a moment as the doctor smiled evilly. But the green was taking over, Silas could barely see as he watched the doctors smile fade.

The one thing the doctor had never witnessed, the one skill that separated Silas from the new mutations. The doctor's surprised face quickly turned to anger as he charged, pulling another dagger from his belt. The doctor leaped into the air, flying straight for Silas, his blood-covered dagger held high.

Silas felt the power in his stomach release as he forced his anger out. His eyes blurred, ten transparent tentacles flew from his eyes and slashed through the doctor before he had even touched the ground.

Again, and again, the tentacles waved, slashing through the doctor until there was nothing left, as he fell to the ground in pieces.

The high-pitched buzzing filled his ears again. Silas pictured the faces of the enemies still fighting.   His hands flew into the air as the tentacles waved violently in triumph. His own yell of victory and agony soared into the heavens. Suddenly, the high-pitched buzzing stopped, the faces around him looked up for one moment before the shock wave erupted, knocking them all into the dust.

Slowly, the tentacles faded, absorbing back into his eyes where they settled – content. Seconds before he collapsed, Silas gazed upon the faces of his brothers, and warriors, all standing amazed, and shocked at the scene before them.

His vision blurred again as the exhaustion swept him away into the peaceful darkness of a dreamless dream.

EPILOGUE

Ten years had passed since that day – the day that the earth ended. Though Silas had considered that day an end to many things, it was also the beginning of everything he knew to be real. He had never expected it to end so suddenly. One day, only a few hours had changed it all, and yet, he still felt sadness when he thought about it.

Silas leaned against the door frame casually as he watched the expanse of field before him. The early morning had become his favorite. Something in the sunlight as it sparkled off the tiny blades of green grass warmed him.

Franklin was a hero to many in the new world. His broadcast to the other sectors had saved thousands, even hundreds of thousands who knew nothing about the portals, or their locations.

Every year, on the anniversary of the end battle – known as *The End Changer* – a celebration was held remembering, and celebrating, those who fought, died, and those who survived the dying planet.

And every year on that day Silas stood staring into the open field under the morning sunlight. He wondered about them, those who remained on NB1. He wondered what had happened after the earth was taken by the fire – after the cave had sealed itself, and the end was final.

The explosion that destroyed half of NB1 was the last he saw of the man-made earth. Since he had recovered from the coma that claimed a year of his life, everything had been different.

The world itself had disappeared. Every part of history, every life that had impacted some other life – it meant nothing.

It was all gone; replaced by some vast unknown planet, and thousands of miles still untouched by man – miles of wilderness untainted and growing freely.

"You can't keep thinking about it you know..." A soft voice floated from behind him. Silas did not turn, he knew the voice well.

"I don't want to forget them." Silas said slowly. "If I've forgotten them, I've forgotten the reason it happened." Vadell placed her small hand on his arm.

"They weren't the only reasons. We all were."

Silas looked at her, she had lost someone too. He felt comforted by the fact that someone understood, someone felt the same sadness that scarred his heart, even after all the years that had passed.

"I'll see you when it's over." She said, patting his arm once before walking out onto the dew-covered lawn.

He watched her depart, disappearing into the distance toward the new city. They were going to make it because they were the lucky ones, the ones who had braved the biggest test of all.

Silas gazed up to the sky, the bluest blue he had ever seen. He doubted the earth had ever been this beautiful, not even at its beginning.

ABOUT THE AUTHOR

BRITTNEY STEWART is the author of "The Last of the Dying" a NaNoWriMo (see nanowrimo.org) 2009 winning novel. Brittney was born and raised in Oklahoma where she lives and writes today.

www.ingramcontent.com/pod-product-compliance
Lightning Source LLC
Chambersburg PA
CBHW022023240626
47154CB00007B/2240